ANIMAL

A MONTANA BOUNTY HUNTERS STORY

DELILAH DEVLIN

ANIMAL

A MONTANA BOUNTY HUNTERS STORY

New York Times and *USA Today* Bestselling Author
Delilah Devlin

Former SEAL, Russell "Animal" Hathcoat, retreated to a remote mountain cabin after leaving the Navy. Haunted by horrific images that replay in his night-mares of his last mission with his SEAL brothers, he intends to renovate the dilapidated cabin as penance and therapy, and to avoid rejoining the world around him. But then, someone who understands what he needs better than he does arrives to offer him a job.

Allie Travers loves the freedom and solitude of being a nature photographer and journalist—until the day she stares through her lens at a charging black bear. With her heart in her throat, she can only stand watching in horror, knowing she'll never escape in time. But rescue comes in the form of a wild man who risks his life to frighten away the animal.

Once the danger is past, she's told by his team of bounty hunters that she has more to fear than any animal in the woods. A felon is on the loose, and she has to accompany them to safety. Seeing an opportu-nity, Allie shadows the team as they hunt their prey deep in a national forest.

Much to Animal's chagrin, more than just his protective instincts are aroused by the pretty photo-journalist.

CHAPTER 1

THE NIGHT AIR was cool and crisp as Brian Cobb rounded the end of his van and pushed on his wheels, powering his chair toward the hunters gathered at the end of a Baptist church's empty parking lot. As good a place as any to meet without drawing too much attention to themselves. They'd decided a face-to-face was needed to pull together everything they'd learned so far about Wayne Tibbets, who a week ago had skipped his date with the judge. Tibbets's charges stemmed from an incident that had occurred near Jewel Basin in the Flathead National Forest, where he'd been pulled over by a park ranger based on the suspicion that he'd been trapping inside the forest. The fact he'd had two dead wolves in his truck bed had escalated the confrontation and left the ranger fighting for his life from multiple gunshot wounds. The ranger had survived, but months later still hadn't recovered enough to return to duty.

Due to the severity of the charges he faced, Tibbets's bail had been set at $600,000. Juicy enough to ensure every bounty hunter in the region was hot-footing it to this remote corner of Montana in hopes of bringing him in.

Brian's agency had the advantage because this was their backyard, and they knew the Tibbets clan only too well. They were frequent "guests" of the local jail, with a long history of theft, poaching, and numerous alcohol-related offenses.

Gathered early this morning beneath a bright parking lot light were Reaper and Carly Stenberg, Dagger Renfrew, Lacey Jones, Cochise Mercier, and Hook Hoecker, Montana Bounty Hunters' latest new hire.

As Brian neared the group, he grinned. Even from twenty feet away, he could hear the agitation in Reaper Stenberg's voice. Since Jamie and Sky had taken an extended leave to sort out their wedding plans, Reaper had been left in charge of the Bear Lodge office. Normally, he gave the hunters autonomy to pick and choose their targets, and then let them scatter to the winds. However, Tibbets was a big fish and all hands were on deck.

"So, you're telling me this jerk-off's a ghost?" he grumbled, raking a hand over his braided blond hair. "A whole damn week in, and we got nada?"

Lacey Jones raised a hand, pretending timidity. The former YouTube makeup maven had proven surprisingly resourceful over the past months since she'd elbowed her way inside MBH, much to her partner Dagger Renfrew's chagrin. On dangerous hunts, he'd just as soon she sat at home and worked on a contour and highlighting video or hosted a beauty party for the "nags" in Bear Lodge. Anything but put herself in the crosshairs. But Lacey was a bit of an adrenaline junkie now. "Reaper, I worked his mom and dad, but they're tough nuts. I mean, really crazy nutjobs—like those Free Montana anarchists we dealt with a while back. I offered the missus a free facial, but she chased me off her porch with a shotgun. Who passes up a free Tatcha face mask?" she said, her eyes widening.

Reaper narrowed his gaze, but the little blonde didn't back up a step, and then she had the additional temerity to point upward at the cross atop the steeple, reminding Reaper where they were.

Brian was convinced Lacey's ditziness was all theater. She was very skilled at the feminine art of distraction. Even her clothing was diverting. Tonight, cotton-candy-pink, faux fur lined the collar and cuffs of her blue-jean jacket. Rhinestone buttons twinkled in the lamplight. But all the bling dimmed beside her pale blonde hair and pretty, confectionary daintiness.

When Reaper gave a low growl, put his hands on his hips, and leaned over her, Brian began to chuckle. The man's jaws ground audibly, and his face turned red, but he bit back whatever string of cusswords he was ready to let loose. Instead, his head swung toward Dagger as if to say, *What the hell is she talking about?*

Dagger lifted both hands. "What she said. The woman turned down a pricey facial—and she really could have used it." He shivered like a girl.

Reaper's lips twisted, and then he started to laugh. "Asshole," he muttered when he recovered.

Dagger reached out and patted his shoulder. "At least we know where he isn't. While Lacey had the old folks at the front door, I slipped through a window and had a quick look around. I found no sign he'd been there." He held up a notebook. "I did find the old lady's address book with notes about who's been naughty and nice for next year's Christmas list." His gaze slipped past Reaper, going to Brian as he came up beside them. Dagger held out the book. "Brian, maybe you could cross-reference the names we already have to see if there are any likely folks who'd be willing to help Wayne."

Brian nodded, not bothering to mention Dagger had entered the house illegally, and reached for the address book, not the least put out by having the administrative task dumped in his lap. This was his life now. Maybe he didn't have legs, but his talents were still needed by this rough and ready crew. His thrills came vicariously, helping them track down the bad guys.

Reaper sighed and turned his attention to Hook. "You find the cousin?"

Murray Tibbets, who'd been fined along with

Wayne earlier that year for hunting deer out of season, hadn't been seen by his manager at the Chicken Hut in Olney since the weekend.

Hook wrinkled his nose. "Cochise and I checked his trailer, his last girlfriend's place, and his favorite bar. A waitress mentioned he had a camper on a creek. We're going to hit the land management office in the morning to see if the Tibbets family has any properties on streams."

Reaper nodded. "Damn, we need more boots on the ground."

Brian cleared his throat. "Spoke to Fetch on the way over. Said he was sending Mace and his dog Taco. He's also got a lead on someone who might be a good fit for our office."

Reaper blew out a breath that filled his cheeks. "Don't need to train any new guy in the middle of this clusterfuck," he muttered.

"Said he's a former SEAL."

All the men grimaced. Carly and Lacey shared sly smiles.

"Sky's a SEAL..." Brian said innocently, knowing none of them had real reservations regarding a SEAL's abilities, but there was already a little inter-service rivalry between the former Marines and Army Rangers in the office. Brian had been a lowly Army MP, not an exalted warrior type, so he didn't have any prejudices.

"Well, we need bodies, I guess," Reaper muttered. "Need more folks combing his haunts and hitting up his friends. But I have a feeling we'll be spending some time in the woods. Tibbets knows the mountains. If he's smart, he'll head cross-country to the border. It's what I'd do." Reaper gave Brian a glance. "You know, you didn't have to come all the way out here to tell us that," he said, his voice gruff. "We all have cellphones."

Brian grimaced. "I know, but I was feeling a little restless. The office has been dead. Besides, who doesn't like a secret rendezvous in the middle of the night?"

"Don't tell a lie," Lacey said, again pointing upward again. "You're just looking for an excuse not to open in the morning. You're avoiding Raydeen."

Brian was glad the shadows hid his blush. The physical therapist had taken to dropping in, almost daily, ostensibly to check on when her running buddy, Hook, was returning. Brian liked Raydeen and thought she was pretty in a healthy sort of way. Tall and muscular. Latte-colored skin, with adorable freckles sprinkled across her nose and cheeks. Thick, curly hair a man would love to wrap around his fist...

Best not to go there. Raydeen had Brian staked out to be her next "project." He dodged her like she had the plague every time he made it to one of the Soldiers' Sanctuary mixers. He wasn't interested in therapy. Didn't want a pair of fake goddamn legs. He was doing just fine in his chair, thank you very much.

"I'll make copies of the entries in the book then slip it into an envelope to mail back to Mrs. Tibbets," he said, giving Dagger a glare to remind him he'd stretched the law entering the Tibbets home without cause.

Dagger grinned.

Brian gave Reaper one last glance. "I'll be in touch. Mace will need to know where to marry up with you guys, and I'll let you know whether Fetch brings that SEAL on board. He'll be heading straight to the field, so I know Fetch won't send you someone who's not ready."

The women moved closer, bent, and gave him hugs. The guys waved or jerked their chins in his direction.

So maybe the trip from Bear Lodge had been a bit of a boondoggle, but rubbing shoulders with the guys who did the dirty work made him feel connected. Needed.

Respected.

He knew he did a lot for the crew—internet searches, cold calls to relatives and friends of skips —but he also paid the bills, answered the phones, and kept the lights on. He was the hub of the operation.

Or at least, he liked to believe that. Jamie told him that often. Based on her recommendation, Fetch had brought him on board, pulling him away from the deep, blue funk he'd fallen into after he'd left Walter Reed.

They'd given him a purpose. Now, he'd never let either of them down or any of the men and women who worked for the agency. Without them, he'd lose every reason he had for existing.

As he waited for his lift to raise him inside the van, he recounted the number of times he'd sat alone in the dark, one drink away from pulling the trigger.

The only thing that had kept him from ending it all had been the thought that Jamie would most likely have been the person who discovered his body—and he'd never do that to his best friend. When she'd taken to leaving her dog, Tessa, with him when she didn't need to bring along a tracking dog, he'd found another reason to live.

Now, Fetch and Reaper relied on him. As annoyed as he'd been, at first, with all the hoops they'd all gone through to find the right office space— a house with an attached apartment for him, ramps and cabinets retrofitted to make the place completely wheelchair accessible—he was grateful. But now, he was also indebted.

Behind the wheel again, he flashed the van's light at the crew still huddled beneath the light. They waved, and he pulled out of the parking lot to head back home. Once on the road, he rolled down the windows to let the wind riffle his hair. In the driver's seat, with a long stretch of road ahead of him, he felt content.

Fetch checked his GPS again then squinted up the mountain, trying to decide whether the rutted dirt trail that spidered up the incline actually led to a cabin. He spotted no electrical poles. No mailbox. He'd been told the former SEAL had gone "native", but this was ridiculous.

He shoved his gear stick into low and pointed his truck up the steep path. At the top of a ridge, he noted several tree stumps. They looked freshly cut, and long logs were piled in a row—the beginning of a clearing in front of a rough, ramshackle cabin. The shingled roof over the porch sank in the middle. The planks of the porch were uneven, and several had buckled. Two windows flanked the front door; one of them was boarded with plywood.

Why the owner hadn't burned the place to the ground and started over mystified him.

But some men liked a challenge. Or needed one to bring focus and purpose to a damaged soul. Something Fetch understood all too well. It was why he'd started Montana Bounty Hunters—to give those bruised souls a purpose and a family. And it was why he was here, looking for one Russell Hathcoat, who was better known among the SEALs as "Animal."

He cut his engine and climbed down from the cab. Then he unbuckled his holster and left it on the seat. No need to give Animal any excuses to think he was a threat, showing up as he was, out of the blue.

He scanned the area and spotted an old pickup parked beneath a lean-to on one side of the cabin. He hoped that meant Animal was home. In the distance, he heard something being smashed or chopped. He followed the sounds around the back of the house and paused.

A tall, massively built man stood bare-chested, holding an axe. In front of his feet were the remains of a piece of furniture, dull knobs glinting on splintered drawers.

"Looks like that cabinet lost the argument," Fetch drawled.

The big man's head swung toward Fetch. Dark eyebrows lowered.

Fetch took in the long tangled hair, the scraggly beard, the pinched mouth, and offered a smile. "You must be Animal."

"What gave it away?" the man rasped and tossed down his axe, a look of disgust twisting his lips.

"A friend of yours gave me some sketchy directions. Said you were living in a rustic cabin." Fetch glanced at the log cabin and back at Animal. "Said you wouldn't take kindly to strangers."

"And yet, you're here." Animal turned to fully face him, his fists curled at his sides.

"He said you might be looking for work."

"He'd be wrong."

Fetch nodded. "Don't imagine you have many expenses out here. Do you even have running water?"

Animal grunted. "I have a generator. It runs the pump when I want to piss." His eyebrows lowered further. "Who the hell are you?"

"I'm Fetch Winters. I run Montana Bounty Hunters. I could use a man with your skills."

Animal's expression shuttered. "You don't want me."

"You're a SEAL."

"*Was*. I walked away."

"Three years shy of retiring..."

"You know your way out of here." Animal turned away and reached for a T-shirt he'd hung on a bush. He donned it then flipped his hair from under the collar. When he glanced back at Fetch, he said, "You're still here?"

Fetch smiled amiably. "We haven't talked. I'd like to tell you about my agency. About the men and women I've employed. The work we do."

"You're wasting your breath," the man growled.

"Maybe, but I brought a six-pack with me. When we've finished it off, I'll go."

Fetch held his breath. If Animal gave him a firm rejection now, he'd leave and never trouble him again. A man had a right to his choices, but he hoped, for Animal's sake, that he was ready to listen.

He'd heard a little about what had led Animal to muster out and retreat to the woods. A mission gone wrong. Friends lost. A lone survivor. Fetch understood the guilt that could eat at a man when he'd lost everyone around him.

He waited, not speaking or changing his expression, giving Animal a chance to decide.

Animal's gaze scanned the view from his little mountaintop. "Guess I didn't get far enough lost," he said under his breath. Then he glanced back at

Fetch. "You didn't bring any European crap, did you?"

Fetch grinned. "Budweiser." He was glad he'd gone for what he himself liked to drink when Animal gave him a nod and led the way around his cabin to the rickety porch.

An hour later, Fetch felt pretty good about his conversation with the SEAL. He picked up his cellphone then frowned. Not until he was back on the highway did he get a signal.

"Hey, boss," Reaper said.

"Heard you're having a hard time hunting down Tibbets."

"He went to ground. His own folks don't have a clue where he's at."

"Mace and Taco make it out there?"

"They did. Arrived bright and early. I sent them with Dagger and Lacey. They'll catch him up with what we know, then carve up the territory they still have to cover." Reaper drew a deep, audible breath. "Heard you were interviewing some new guy."

"Interviewed and hired him."

Fetch could well imagine what was going through the other man's head right about then. Relief at having another body to beat the bushes for their target, but leery over the fact a stranger would be joining his already tight little community of hunters. Just as he'd hoped when he'd asked Jamie and Reaper to set up a satellite office, they'd built a strong, seamless team.

"Hope he's not expecting any new employee orientation," Reaper muttered.

Fetch grinned. "He's quiet, and he hasn't been out long."

"Is he twitchy?"

"I believe he's solid, but he's got a few ghosts to get past."

"Don't we all?"

"Yeah, well, he's got your number. He'll make his way to Olney this afternoon."

"Carly and I will be sure to keep close to town."

"Tell that pretty wife of yours hello from me."

"Hi, Fetch!" she sang out in the background.

"You ever finish that book?" he asked, grinning because he'd known when he'd sent her to ride along with Reaper that her days as a romance author were likely numbered. Reaper had been ready to settle down. Carly was a wholesome beauty and strong-willed enough to put up with Reaper's badass attitude.

So, maybe he'd been matchmaking. Everything had worked out fine, and he'd added another hunter to his payroll.

She laughed. "I haven't written a word in months. But you probably know that."

"I'm happy for you both."

Reaper grunted in his ear. "Anything else, boss, besides giving me a hard time?"

"Nope. I wish you luck. Tibbets needs to be

taken down. Let me know if you need anything else from me."

"Out here."

As the call ended, Fetch turned on the radio. A mournful-sounding George Strait song was playing. "Yeah, George, take me home."

CHAPTER 2

Animal tuned out the crackling, thudding sounds of his team members moving through the forest.

On day three after he'd joined the hunt, he wasn't regretting his decision to give MBH a try. He'd been unwilling to make any long-term promises. Hadn't signed a contract or filled out a W-9. Not yet, anyway. When Fetch had described what Tibbets had done, and then talked about the hunters who were already on his trail, Animal had felt a stirring of interest. Manhunts were something he was familiar with. So, he wasn't hunting a high-dollar target through the Hindu Kush mountains. Wasn't dropping into some walled compound to sweep a house in the dead of night.

Still, this felt familiar. Moving through the bushes. Tracking a target. Looking for campfires, footprints, signs Tibbets had stopped to piss or shit.

That morning, they'd found a butchered deer. Most of the carcass had been picked apart by scavengers. So, it hadn't been left by a game hunter. He'd taken a portion of a haunch, had roasted it over a quickly built fire, and had eaten as much as he could before moving on.

Looked like Tibbets was feeling pretty sure he'd slipped the noose. He hadn't even bothered to try to bury the evidence he'd been there.

The first afternoon, Animal had ridden along with Carly and Reaper. They'd shown him the warrant and pictures of Tibbets and his family. They'd canvassed businesses in Olney—gun shops, grocers, gas stations, but no one recalled seeing him or his cousin Murray.

That evening, they headed to Tibbets's favorite haunt again. The women sat at the long polished bar, chatting up the bartender and the waitresses. Dagger and Mace played pool with two plugged-in and gossipy locals. Reaper and Animal sat at a table, watching the doors. But none of them were getting any bites.

About an hour into their surveillance, Hook and Cochise arrived.

Hook slapped a map on the table. "Found the parcel his family owns. It sits on a creek."

"'Bout damn time," Reaper had muttered.

The next morning, they'd geared up and surrounded a small, ratty camper trailer. Tibbets had been there recently but was now gone. After tearing through his belongings, searching for clues where he might have gone next, they bagged up dirty clothes for Mace's dog Taco to scent on.

The moment Taco lowered his nose to the ground, following Tibbets's trail from the camper's metal steps, they'd realized the man had headed straight into the woods, afoot, rather than driving out.

They'd left Dagger, Lacey, and Cochise behind to watch for any movement in town, and to keep an eye out for any of his relatives who looked ready to head north with supplies to help him out. The rest of the team members grabbed their gear from their vehicles and began tracking Tibbets into Flathead National Forest.

Animal didn't mind the rough conditions. He was accustomed to long marches and sleeping on the ground. None of the hunters, even Carly Stenberg, complained about the conditions, even after they'd endured a chilly rain the previous day. They'd dried their clothes beside a fire last night, reasonably assured they were still a day's hike from catching up to Tibbets. Conversation had flowed around him, but he hadn't felt the need to try to contribute.

This was a tight, well-trained crew, and they knew each other well. But they seemed to understand he wasn't the chatty type. He rather liked the fact they let him be.

They came to the edge of the woods. A large meadow stretched before them, mountains in the background. The meadow was broken on one side by ridges of exposed rock.

"We got company," Reaper said quietly. They all held back, remaining hidden in the brush. Reaper lifted an arm and pointed.

Animal pulled out his tactical telescope and followed Reaper's direction, at last spotting a slender figure standing beside an outcropping. Not their mark. A woman. She stood in front of a tripod and peered into a camera. She had wheat-colored hair drawn back into a messy braid. She wore a red plaid shirt and a khaki vest over blue jeans and boots.

Suddenly, she jerked back her head, giving him a glimpse of her profile. Her eyebrows were lowered, her mouth dropping as she stared down the hill.

He turned his telescope toward whatever had caught her attention and immediately understood her concern.

A baby black bear ambled into the clearing, heading upward toward her location.

"Where's mama?" he whispered.

As though answering his question, a loud bellow sounded from the forest farther down the tree line. A large bear ran out, huffing and bellowing, heading toward the woman.

He didn't have even a millisecond to think through a better plan. Animal dumped his pack and ran into the clearing, tearing at his shirt. When he'd ripped off the buttons down the front, he flapped the edges, trying to make himself look bigger. "Ha! Ha!"

he yelled as loud as he could to draw the bear's attention away from the woman.

Mama bear bounced on her front paws and spun toward him.

"Don't shoot unless you have to!" Animal tossed over his shoulder to Reaper.

"Don't get in my line of fire!" Reaper shouted back.

"Don't shoot her!" the woman screamed.

"You shut up!" Animal yelled, still running, still flapping. Didn't she realize he was trying to draw the bear's attention *away* from her?

The bear's head moved from Animal, to Reaper behind him, and again to the woman, likely trying to decide who was the biggest danger to her cub.

Animal roared and flapped and moved a little closer.

The baby bear squalled and changed direction, running for his mama.

Just when Animal feared the bear would charge, she spun and ran into the woods, her cub running right behind her.

Animal halted, breathing hard. He gave another flap of his shirt. "Ha! Ha!" he shouted, hoping she'd been startled bad enough not to turn around.

Then he heard a whirring sound, coming from up the rise. He turned his head toward the woman. The sound came from her camera. Animal gave her a fierce glare then began to stalk up the rise.

When he reached her, she straightened and

flashed him a wide smile. "Thanks for that. Thought for a second there I was going to be lunch."

"What the hell!" he bellowed, anger shot through him. Didn't she have a clue how close to being "lunch" he'd been, trying to rescue her? And all she'd thought about was taking her damn pictures?

Her eyebrows shot upward, and she stood still.

Behind him, he heard more of his team stomping up the hill. He should have turned and walked away. Should have let Reaper handle getting her packed up and off the mountain. Away from him.

Instead, anger vibrated through him. He glanced at the gear strewn around her feet. "Who the hell comes out to the wilderness without a goddamn gun?"

"The only shots I plan to take are with my camera," she said icily, lifting her chin.

He ground his teeth as his face heated.

"Wish I'd been shooting video though," she said. "The footage would've gone viral. Do you chase bears often?"

He narrowed his gaze, not liking her smartass tone. Did she know how close he was to exploding? Men he'd fought with knew better than to talk to him when he was like this.

A throat cleared beside him. "Ma'am, you need to pack up," Reaper said, his voice even.

Her hazel gaze darted from Animal to the man standing beside him. "Why? She's gone."

"The bear's the least of what you have to worry about out here."

She seemed to finally take in the fact that she was surrounded by five well-armed strangers. "Were you tracking her?"

"We don't hunt bear," Reaper said, his voice lowering.

Animal felt a little of his steam begin to cool hearing Reaper's clipped delivery. Someone else here got the fact she had no business out here. Alone.

"Well, I thank you for your advice, but I have no intention of packing up and leaving. It took me three days to get here. I'll be setting up camp." She bent and swiped at the straps of her backpack then reached inside it. She pulled out a small 9mm Colt Defender but had the good sense to point it away from the group. "I'm not unarmed."

Animal grunted. "Think that would have stopped her? If you didn't hit her in the head, you'd just piss her off."

"Well, that's not your worry, is it?" Again, she lifted her chin.

Damn, if his body didn't go hard. The way she locked her gaze with his, she didn't show any fear. Foolish was what she was. He could get around her gun and have her on the ground in the time it took her to realize he'd even moved.

"This is no place for a woman on her own, not today," Reaper said.

Her back stiffened. Her cheeks paled just a bit.

"We're not what you should fear," Carly said quickly, stepping past Animal and Reaper. "It's gonna take a few minutes for these two get over the adrenaline rush to explain. I'm Carly," she said, reaching out her hand.

The woman passed the gun from her right to her left and shook Carly's hand. "Carly, it's nice to meet you." She didn't smile, and her gaze kept scanning the rest of them, like she expected them to make a move against her.

Animal drew a deep breath. He knew what she saw. He wasn't into scaring women. Happened naturally, often enough. He set his hands on his hips and glanced at the ground while he waited for the tension in his body to ease.

"We're bounty hunters," Carly said. "We've been tracking a dangerous felon. He's in this area. It's not safe for you to be here."

As Animal glanced up again, the woman's frown deepened. "I've been here a day. Haven't seen anyone but you. How do I even know you're telling me the truth?"

Carly glanced back at Reaper. "Show her the warrant."

Reaper reached into his pack and pulled out the folder. He passed it to the woman.

She held the folder in the crook of the arm and thumbed through the documents. "Okay, so I believe you're what you say. But since you're on his trail, and he's not here, why do I have to leave? Obviously, he's already passed my location."

"Because there are going to be more bounty hunters out here, combing the area. We've got the jump on everyone else. When other teams arrive, our skip might double back to evade them. No place in this wilderness is safe."

Her lips thinned then twisted. Her gaze went back to Animal. "Dammit, I just got here."

Animal stepped forward, using his body to intimidate her. Yeah, he felt no shame doing that. Not when scaring her into making the right choice could keep her safe. "You're not safe on your own. Pack up."

Damned if the woman's mouth didn't twitch like she wanted to laugh.

He glared.

She arched a brow. "You're right. It's not safe to be alone out here."

Her expression gave him no ease. He narrowed his eyes until they were slits as he waited for what else she intended to say, because there was no way in hell she was giving up so easily.

She gave a little shrug and grinned. "I'll go with you."

"Hell no," he growled.

"Um, that might be her safest bet," Hook drawled from somewhere behind him.

Animal turned his head and aimed a blistering glare his way.

"You'll have to keep up," Reaper said, not sounding the least bit happy.

"I'm an experienced hiker," she said. "I'll lighten my pack, seeing as I'm not setting up camp here." She backed away from Animal then knelt beside her pack. She unzipped it and began tossing out clothes, notebooks, a small pup tent, and a large baggie of food.

"We've only got rations for ourselves," Animal ground out.

"I packed enough for a week. Did you?"

"We've got enough for two more days," Carly said, her tone too cheerful.

"Fine, I have plenty left." Then she zipped her gun into her pack and walked to her tripod, which she quickly folded and slipped into the larger compartment of her pack. The fancy camera went into a padded case and was also zipped away. From a side pocket, she drew out a small camera dangling from a long cord, which she slipped over her neck.

"We're not stopping for you to take pictures of the views," Animal said, feeling as though steam was about to come out of his ears, his head was so hot.

"Didn't think you would," she said, and gave him a measured smile.

There was a challenge in her eyes, like she wanted him to push back against her intentions again, but he knew this was a game he wouldn't win. The team seemed set on her accompanying them. For her safety.

Why did he have the sneaking suspicion the woman could take care of herself quite well? Had to be the fact she hadn't betrayed an ounce of fear—not when facing an angry bear or a large, angry man.

He raked a hand over his head. "Suit yourself," he muttered.

"I will," she said, so softly he knew he was the only one meant to hear her words.

That nailed it for him. She was one of *those* women—the ones who always had to have the last word in any argument. He spun on his heel and gave a nod to Mace.

Mace held the baggie with Tibbets's smelly clothing in front of Taco, and the dog buried his nose in it. His tail wagged, and his feet pranced, a sign the indefatigable dog was eager to take up the trail again.

Then they were off, moving quickly, because Taco was sniffing the air and pulling against his leash.

They moved at a fast clip, crossing the meadow to enter the woods again on the far side, and then descending into a deep gully.

Animal slid sideways in wet leaves to the bottom, then moved out, not stopping to see how the woman fared or to lend her a hand. She'd wanted to be with them, she'd have to follow under her own steam.

Behind him, he heard the low murmurs of the women talking. It occurred to him they hadn't shared introductions. Which cheered him. At least she'd know they weren't here to make friends or roast marshmallows, although he had a bag tucked in the bottom of his pack. No way would he dig them out now. He had a sweet tooth, but he didn't want to show the woman any softness. The sooner she decided to head to the road to find a ride back to civilization, the better.

Animal didn't want to worry about her. Didn't want to think about what someone like Tibbets and his kin might do when he was cornered. The hunters knew the score. Carly was ex-military herself and had spent time in the desert, so she'd seen the worst a man could do. No, it wasn't the fact the blonde was a woman that caused him problems.

He didn't like that her tanned skin, slim body, and pale wheat hair were appealing. He'd gone a long time without a woman. He didn't like that she made him think about just how long it had been. Hell, it had been since before his last tour. After he'd returned, he hadn't been fit to be around a woman. Hadn't spoken to anyone unless asked a direct question. He still didn't like to talk. The last time he'd felt comfortable, happy enough to shoot the breeze, had been before the battle near Hajin, when his team had sat in a hangar, waiting for helicopters to drop them in the desert to support Iraqi forces battling ISIS in that godforsaken corner of Syria. They'd talked about their kids, their vacation plans. Animal and Jessie Forte had planned to head to Bermuda to swim with sharks.

But he'd lost the friends he'd known and trained with for years. They'd been family. Their families had been family. All that was gone now. He'd been the only one to walk away, and he still didn't understand how the rounds that had exploded, decimating his teammates, had managed to leave him with barely a scratch.

Animal forced his thoughts away from that last battle. No use reliving it again. He visited those blood-soaked sands every night in his dreams. Just as well he hadn't sought out a woman. What if he fell asleep? He wasn't sure if she'd feel his fists or hear his whimpers. Neither scenario was one he was willing to risk.

Up ahead, Taco paused and lowered his head to sniff at the ground, left and right, then moved forward again. He'd caught Tibbets's trail, not just a hint of his scent wafting on the breeze. Taco moved forward again, this time more slowly until he moved right to climb up the side of the ravine, but Mace held him back. "Look," he called out softly, pointing at the rocky wall of the ravine.

There were grooves on the side, along with partial prints from the soles of boots. A man, maybe two, had climbed and slid downward, then clawed their way upward, and from the looks of the wet mud at the edges of the grooves, not long ago.

Mace unclipped Taco from his leash and gave him a hand signal to climb the side of the ravine. The dog circled back then ran for the side, digging in his nails to climb, reaching the top then turning to wait for Mace.

Animal cupped his hands and bent. "It'll be quicker if I boost you up, past the slurry at the bottom."

Mace nodded and placed a boot in Animal's hands. Animal jerked upward, propelling him toward a rocky outcrop that provided him the handhold he needed to climb the rest of the way up. Animal did the same for Carly, who reached out with her other hand for Mace to help her up.

Reaper raised an eyebrow. Taller than Animal, Reaper simply jumped to reach the outcropping then hauled himself up and over the edge.

Animal boosted Hook then turned to the woman.

She didn't say a word, just set her small foot in his cupped hands. He jerked her upward. Her arm flailed, stretching toward the outcropping and wrapping only the ends of her fingers over the edge. Knowing she needed more of a boost, he reached out and clapped his palms on her ass to push her higher until Mace caught her outstretched hand.

When Animal scrambled up the side, her cheeks were red, and she gave him a glare.

He didn't bother hiding a smirk. Yeah, her firm ass had felt nice against his palms, and maybe she hadn't needed all the extra help, but this time, he'd liked having the "last word."

CHAPTER 3

ALLISON TRAVERS barely resisted the urge to reach back and rub her bottom. Beneath her jeans, her skin burned where he'd clamped his large hands and manhandled her up the ravine wall. How dare he? And he was grinning about it! *Ooh!* How she wanted to slap the smile right off his face, but then she'd have to touch him.

And good Lord, once she did, she wasn't sure she could stop. Her fingers tingled at the prospect. She'd never seen a man like him. Big and hairy. His chest still bared because he hadn't bothered changing his shirt after he'd popped all his buttons to flap the garment at a charging bear.

Despite the fact she'd been scared spitless the second she'd spotted Mama Bear, she hadn't been able to take her gaze off the crazy man rushing into the field. She'd immediately ducked behind her camera to film the whole damn thing. And she'd lied, because she'd switched to video to capture the entire incident. Who would believe her otherwise? The second the bear had high-tailed it into the brush, she'd switched back to take stills, one after another, of the dark, feral, bearded man striding up the hill toward her.

Damn, she'd had a moment standing there, when she'd wondered whether she should run away herself, but she wasn't made that way—sensible, cautious. Instead, she'd stiffened her spine.

The second she had, his dark eyes had narrowed to icy slivers. She'd shivered at that look, but since there were others, some smiling and heading her way, she'd figured they'd step in. So, she hadn't worried too much about continuing to anger him.

Besides, he fascinated her. That large, powerful frame, the wild hair and eyes. He was more primal than the creatures she'd come to photograph.

And now, he was stomping behind her, nearly on her heels, willing her to hurry up, but that only goaded her to slow her pace and sway her hips.

At the low growl she heard behind her, she grinned. So, he'd noticed. Good. This change of plans, following the hunters while they hunted a human prey, might prove to be even more lucrative than the photographs of bears, wolves, and eagles she'd hoped to sell. They'd go along nicely with the article she'd write about the rough and ready team she now shadowed. Her opening paragraphs would describe the moment a wild man chased a bear into the forest, facing him with nothing but his bare chest and hands.

And who wrote about bounty hunters? She'd have the corner on this underrepresented profession. Surely, some man's magazine dedicated to armchair warriors would love to read a real-life thrill ride. Already, she'd surreptitiously shot a couple dozen photographs of the team as they moved efficiently through the brush. She hoped she was still with them when they apprehended Tibbets. No way would she willingly let them leave her behind. This could be the scoop of a lifetime.

"We're falling behind," said her surly escort.

"Worried you'll get lost in the woods?" she said airily, not looking back although she craved seeing his expression.

"Huh." He brushed past her and walked quickly to close the distance with the rest of the team.

She would have whistled, if she'd had the extra air. Picking up her pace, she realized she wasn't as well-conditioned as the others. Which surprised her, because she'd always been fit and lean. Although, thinking about it, she had been pretty sedentary of late, writing and diligently combing through and editing thousands of photos she'd shot on her trip through the Everglades last fall.

The view in front of her kept her from grumbling too much about the fact she was bringing up the rear. The big guy's rear end was barely visible beneath his large pack, but his thick thighs and broad frame were...inspiring.

Allie shook her head. Her taste in men was deplorable. She would have thought after she'd dated the Everglades park ranger, she would have learned that big and silent usually masked a miniscule brain. The bounty hunter probably spent his off-time hunting the creatures she loved or drinking beer until the wee hours with his redneck buddies.

But he was healthy. Had all his teeth and a full head of hair. The fact she'd never kissed a bearded man tickled her imagination. What would that feel like?

Oh stop! she scolded herself. Now was not the time to fantasize. They had a criminal to catch. She had photos to take, and doing that on the move provided its own complications. She preferred setting up her equipment, sitting still in nature until the animals crossed her view. Sure, she hunted, looking for likely spots to catch glimpses of her prey, like the wide grassland she'd selected where deer and their predators would come. Her larger aperture camera allowed her to capture breathtaking, panoramic vistas. Stuck with her little Canon Sure Shot, she'd have to pray for the right light at the right moment. But beggars couldn't be choosers. The last thing she could ask of her escorts was for them to hold still while she snapped away.

The thought of asking the big guy in front of her

to stare fiercely into the distance while she circled him, made her chuckle.

He shot a glare over his shoulder, and she wiped away her smile.

This hunt they were on was serious business. Tibbets was a hardcore, dangerous criminal. She'd better keep that in the forefront of her mind. She'd shadow the team, keeping as quiet as she could so as not to distract them, and maybe they'd forget she was even there.

Skipping to catch up, she didn't worry about what came next, not the next shot or even when they'd break to eat and use the "facilities". She trained her focus on the team. She had a lot to learn. Starting with all their names. She knew Carly's and her husband Reaper's, but that was all. First stop, she'd be sure to note all of them, just to make sure she got the attributions right for her articles. She'd decided bounty hunters were worth at least a series.

LUNCH WAS SPENT JUST below a high ridgeline to prevent their bodies from appearing silhouetted from below. Still, they were high enough they had a view of treetops.

Reaper frowned. "No smoke. Would be nice if he'd stop to rest and cook a meal to give us a chance to catch up."

Carly sat down beside Allie, munching on a

protein bar. "How are you holding up? I know the guys set a brisk pace."

Allie wrinkled her nose. "I thought I was in decent shape."

The other woman grinned. "Yeah, well if you need to hand over your backpack to lighten your load, don't hesitate. They won't mind."

"I'm good," she said, wishing she was a little less stubborn, but she didn't want to give the big guy a reason to force her to leave. She wasn't asking for any special treatment, even if it killed her. She cleared her throat. "It'd help knowing everyone's names…"

Carly nodded. "Sorry about that. Here you are traipsing through the woods with folks you don't know. Has to be a little unnerving."

"I'm surprisingly okay with this. After what happened with the bear, the rest of this has been pretty tame. However, it would help to know every-one's names."

Carly grinned and eased her back against a tree. "Well, you already know Reaper and me. He's an ex-Marine by the way. I was Army. We're all ex-mili-tary." She pointed toward the well-built man with the prosthetic arm. "That's Hook. He was an Army Ranger and was our latest hire."

"Hook?" Allie cringed a little at the nickname. "He doesn't mind?"

Carly smiled and shook her head. "He says it's his life's greatest irony. His last name's Hoecker, and his teammates called him Hook. After his injury, it was a little rough for a while, but he's adapted well to the prosthetic. Considers it his secret weapon now." She nodded toward the man with the German shepherd. "That's Mace. He's on loan from the Kalispell office—we're out of Bear Lodge. Mace's dog's name is Taco, and they were both with the Green Berets. And lastly, there's...Animal." Her gaze was on the big, hairy guy.

Allie's eyebrows rose. The nickname suited him all too well.

"He was a SEAL. Don't know his story yet," Carly said, wrinkling her nose. "He hasn't talked a lot since he joined us three days ago." She darted a glance at Allie. "He's talked to you more than he has the entire team put together."

"Guess I'm just lucky," Allie said dryly.

"I think you get under his skin," Carly whispered. "From what I can tell, that's not a bad thing."

"Huh." Allie pursed her lips. "Have to wonder what's under all that hair."

Carly grinned.

"When he ran out to confront that bear..." Allie drew a deep breath. "For a second, I thought I was being punked. I mean, who does that?"

Carly laughed. "Reaper was staring down his scope at the bear. He'd have taken her down if she'd charged."

"I'm glad he didn't have to," Allie said, shivering.

"Me, too." Carly raised her eyebrows. "So, what's your story?"

Animal finished heating his MRE using the flameless heater that came inside the pack. Tearing off the top of his meal pouch, he moved until he found a tree not already being used and leaned his back against it.

So, maybe he'd chosen his seat because it was near the women, but he was curious about what they were talking about. Their heads were too close together, and they shared too many smiles. Carly was likely dishing on the team to the photographer.

Or that was what he assumed she was. Who else would be in the middle of nowhere with a pricy camera, looking cool as a cucumber after a bear had entered her sights?

"So, what's your story?" he heard Carly say.

Their backs were to him, so he didn't bother pretending his attention wasn't on them. He leaned closer to hear them as he scooped chicken and rice from his pouch.

"I'm a photojournalist."

"That sounds exciting."

She shrugged. "I guess it sounds glamorous. And I do travel quite a bit. Mostly, I'm trekking through mud or sand, looking for the perfect shot. My trip here was supposed to be pretty tame. I live in Helena, but I've rarely visited this part of Montana, and it's right in my backyard."

"So, are you published?" Carly asked.

"I am," she said, nodding. "Mostly wildlife magazines, the occasional birder mag. Once, I made it into National Geographic, but that's a really tough gig to score. I only got my photos in because I was invited by a friend to be part of one of their sponsored expeditions. He submitted a few of mine along with his."

Animal frowned, thinking they had to be more than friends for the guy to do something like that for her. Not his business though. He took another bite, although his stomach was starting to burble. He hoped he had some antacids in the bottom of his pack.

"If I have any good photos from this park," the woman said, "I might try to submit them to the park. Maybe they'd use them in their promo materials, or I'll write an article for *Montana Outdoors*. Hell, I'll probably do both."

"You know, Allie, I'm a writer, too. Strictly fiction though. Or at least, I was."

So, her name was Allie. Good to know, although Allie sounded a little too sweet for her.

Still, he'd grown tired of thinking of her as "the woman" or "the blonde".

"Really? A writer? You burn out or something?"

Carly laughed. "No, I did a ride along with a bounty hunter and got hooked."

"What did you write?"

Carly leaned closer to the woman. "Erotic romance," she whispered.

Animal nearly choked on his food and coughed.

The women glanced over their shoulders at him.

Carly gave him a sly smile. "Oh, I haven't given up writing it entirely. I've been in research mode for months."

Allie laughed. "The kind of research Reaper can help you with?"

Animal rolled his eyes. He knew the two were having fun at his expense. His reddening cheeks gave away the fact he'd heard exactly what she'd said.

Reaper plopped down on the ground beside him. "What'd I miss?"

Carly widened her eyes. "Allie, here, is a photojournalist. It's kind of nice to meet another writer."

"You didn't tell her what you write, did you?" Reaper said, grimacing.

"Sure did. Haven't told her my penname, yet."

Reaper sighed. "She hasn't published since she joined our agency."

"So, you don't have anything to worry about, do you?" Allie said, her eyes glinting wickedly.

Animal's shoulders shook, and he shot a glance at Reaper.

Reaper was giving him a narrow-eyed glare. "Didn't know you could smile."

"I'm not," Animal said, frowning.

"Who could tell if you were?" Allie said, eyeing his beard.

Animal made a growling sound to warn her off, but the smart-alecky woman only smiled.

Reaper blew out a breath. "We need to hit the trail. You about done?"

Animal glanced into his half-eaten packet. His appetite was gone anyway. "I'll pack away my trash," he said, scooping out the remains of his lunch for the critters to eat.

He pushed up from the ground and reached out a hand toward Allie to help her up.

She eyed his hand.

He felt foolish now but didn't withdraw it. Why the heck had he made the gesture?

When she slid her hand inside his, he had his answer. Her palm was warm and smooth. He enclosed it gently and tugged her to her feet.

She gave a low groan. "Damn, and it's only noon?" she muttered under her breath.

"Once you get moving, the kinks will ease," he said gruffly.

She gazed up at him, blinking. Maybe she was surprised by his tone or the fact he hadn't used her momentary show of weakness to remind her she didn't belong there. He knew better than to say anything else. He'd only put his foot in his mouth again. He kind of liked the way she stared back at him, searching his eyes with a little blush creeping across her sun-kissed cheeks.

"Thanks," she said, easing her hand from inside his.

Before she had a chance to complain, he reached down for her pack, slung it over one shoulder, and walked toward Mace who was, once again, refreshing Taco's nose with a boost of scent from Tibbets's dirty clothes.

"Told you they wouldn't mind," Carly said behind him.

Animal had no clue what she was referring to, but he kept his gaze straight ahead. He didn't know why he'd grabbed her pack.

Only, that was a lie. He'd wanted to please her.

Animal frowned. The impulse that had nudged him to act like a gentleman was one he needed to ignore. The last thing he needed to do was entertain the idea of allowing this woman into his life. For the same reason he didn't want her here, he couldn't begin to think of her in a romantic way. He wanted her safe. From Tibbets. From him. Besides, she was way out of his league.

He pushed the troubling thoughts out of his mind. He had a job to do. Whether or not he accepted Fetch's offer of permanent employment was a decision he'd defer until the end of this hunt as well. For now, he was losing focus, letting the woman crawl under his skin and imagining that she was interested in him in a way other than as a story to pursue.

How unlucky could a man be to have the one woman on the planet who'd stirred heat inside him in a long, long time, and her not return that interest? If he believed in God, he might think the Almighty was having a great laugh at his expense.

The team continued their trek, Mace and Taco on point, the rest fanning out in the woods, looking for signs of Tibbets. Taco spent most of his time with his nose up, scenting the air. He'd lost the stronger-scented trail of Tibbets's footsteps shuffling on the ground. Nearing dusk, when the sun backlit the forest in a golden blaze, Mace pulled on Taco's leash then raised a closed fist.

The group halted, remaining silent.

Animal sniffed the air. *There.* He hadn't imagined it. The smell of roasting meat drifted over him. Someone's campfire was close by.

The group gathered. Mace kept a loose hand around Taco's snout to calm him, so he didn't whine and give away their presence.

Reaper leaned into the huddle. "We'll wait until dusk. We'll still have enough light to navigate, but the shadows will be deeper. We'll stand a better chance of getting close before he knows he's surrounded."

"Damn, I hope it's him," Carly whispered. "My feet are ready for long soak."

Reaper gave her a tight smile. "Hunker down, for now. We have maybe twenty minutes. Check your weapons. Be ready."

Carly dug into her backpack and withdrew a small plastic case. She opened it to reveal small communications earpieces then passed the case around. Everyone took a one before passing the case back to Carly, including Allie, who stared at the small skin-toned device.

Animal leaned toward her, holding up his earpiece. "This is the switch," he said, touching the small black switch on the top. "When it's time, turn it on. No need to use up the battery now."

"Thanks," she said, closing it inside her hand.

"When we move out, you plant your ass someplace safe," he said, locking his gaze with hers to let her know he was dead serious.

She nodded. "I'm not looking to get caught up in the middle of your takedown. This is your expertise, not mine."

"Good." He gave her a little smile. "When we're done, we'll come back for you."

She tossed back her head. "Think I'd let you forget me?"

His gaze swept her upturned face, but he didn't answer. His tongue felt strangely heavy, and he knew whatever garbled thing he'd manage to say would sound stupid. So, instead, he gave her a quick nod.

Twenty minutes crawled by. The shadows deepened around them.

When Reaper pushed to his feet, the rest of the team did too. Once again, Mace led with Taco, who panted and whose body quivered with excitement.

They moved swiftly through the trees, following the dog, then separating the moment a flickering flame appeared between branches.

They surrounded the camp.

"I see our target," Hook whispered, "beside the fire."

"Any sign of the cousin?" Reaper asked.

"Lying down," Carly said.

Animal crouched and moved closer, waiting for the signal for the team to converge on Wayne and Murray Tibbets, eager to end this and get the woman to safety.

CHAPTER 4

ALLIE KNEW she was being foolish. Worse, she was betraying Animal. She'd promised to "plant" herself well away from the action. But here she was, her Sigma lens set to a wide aperture, hoping she'd get some decent shots, but knowing that night photography was not her forte. Likely, if the team moved fast, all she'd capture was gray streaking figures.

Well, she was hunkered down at an angle from the rest of the group. She'd edged around the clearing as quietly as she could, given she'd moved on her hands and knees to keep from being seen.

Now, she lay on her belly, resting on an elbow with her camera cupped on her palm. With the flash off, she took several shots of the Tibbets. Wayne sat in front of the fire, turning what looked like a rabbit on a makeshift spit, while his cousin played a game on his cellphone. The sounds of bells and music were incongruous, given where they were and what was about to happen.

Allie paused to wipe her sweaty hand on her vest then lowered her eye to the viewfinder again. She didn't see the team, which was a good thing, she hoped.

She'd heard them talking quietly in her ear as they'd surrounded the encampment. Had kept well behind so she knew where they weren't, then moved to this location, bedding down on prickly vines.

Her heart pounded, and she drew slow, deep breaths to calm herself. The team knew what they were doing. She took comfort from that thought, but then she remembered Animal's wild run. He'd been completely unconcerned over the fact the bear could have ripped him to shreds with a single swipe of her huge paw. Sure, Allie knew he'd done it to save her, but would he be any less reckless without worrying over some "civilian" in the line of fire? Thank God, he didn't know she was so close, watching the action about to go down. She flipped the switch on her camera to video mode.

"Wayne Tibbets, we have you surrounded!" Reaper shouted out, breaking the silence.

Allie winced at the volume in her ear but kept her gaze glued to Tibbets, who stiffened. His hand reached sideways.

"He's going for a gun!" she squealed.

"Goddammit, woman!" Animal rasped in her ear.

"Go, go, go!" someone else said, and suddenly the clearing was filled with figures rushing in.

Tibbets rolled to his side and came up on one knee, a shotgun held in front of him. "Take one more step, and I'll shoot the blonde in the grass," he said, swinging his gun toward her.

Out of reflex, her finger stayed pressed against the camera's shutter button, as she stared right at Tibbets. Hell, she'd thought she'd hidden herself better than that.

"We don't want anyone hurt," Reaper said, his voice deepening.

The ominous note made Allie shiver. Why wasn't Tibbets doing the same? His eyes narrowed as he sighted down his barrel.

Allie knew the man didn't care whether she lived or died. She was pretty sure he didn't care about his own hide either. He would fight rather than be taken into custody. The moment stretched, her looking at the end of his barrel, the silence so deep she swore she heard Tibbets's breaths from over twenty feet away.

Someone had to do something to break the stand-off. So, she did the only thing she could think to do, she rolled quickly to her right.

A shot whizzed by, and she gasped, not stopping her roll until she hit a tree. Pain exploded in her head, and she cried out.

"Goddammit!" Animal shouted.

He really needed a bigger repertoire of curse

words, she thought, cupping the side of her head and feeling warmth and wetness trickle through her fingers. Holy hell, had she been shot?

The sounds of gunfire quickly stilled, followed by flesh thumping flesh, and then a body landed beside her, and she closed her eyes, wishing she'd done as she'd promised and stayed put, because then she wouldn't be about to die.

Fingers pried hers away from the side of her head.

"We got him!" Hook called out.

"Now, Murray, you know you don't want to do anything stupid," Reaper warned.

The sounds of a scuffle ensued, but Allie rolled to her back and looked up at Animal's big frame. Even in the darkness, she knew it was him.

He knelt on one knee beside her. "Baby, what'd you do?" he asked.

Then a light shone, nearly blinding her. "I got shot," she said, her voice quivering.

More lights shone, and she watched as Carly and Mace knelt beside her.

Animal's expression wasn't what she expected. There was no sorrow, no deep concern, just a quizzical look in his eyes and slight smile. Well, hell. Did her imminent death mean so little to him?

He cleared his throat. "Sweetheart, you're not shot. You hit your head on the tree. You have a nasty cut, but I think you'll live."

His tone went a long way toward mollifying her.

It was soft. Sexy.

She drew a deep breath then pushed up on her elbows. Her head swam, and she lay down again.

"Don't know how you didn't knock yourself out," Animal muttered.

"We've got them secured," Reaper called out. "Allie okay?"

"She'll be fine," Animal said, not glancing away from her.

Carly held out a canteen, a bandana, and a large bandage.

Animal took the items and gently cleaned the wound on the side of her head.

"Sorry. I was so silly," she said. "I should have stayed back."

"Yes, you should have."

She held up her camera. "Thought I was well-hidden. I only wanted some shots."

"I figured that out." He wiped again at her temple, and then peeled open a bandage and applied it. "You'll have a nasty bruise."

"And a headache," she croaked.

"That, too."

"Guess this is as good a place as any to make camp tonight," Reaper said in the distance.

Animal grunted. "Yeah, I don't think Allie's in any shape to move tonight."

"I'm sorry," she said, feeling small and stupid. Not a feeling she was familiar with.

"Should be. Scared the shit out of me. We'll talk

about that another time."

"Really?" she asked, because she hadn't been sure until he said it that he'd want to have anything to do with a woman stupid enough to nearly spoil their little operation.

"Think you can sit up now?"

She reached out, but he ignored her hand and gripped her shoulders to lift her torso. He angled her body so she sat with her back against the tree. "Feel dizzy?"

She gently shook her head then wrinkled her nose. "No. I think I was just...panicked. Not something I feel very often."

Carly pushed up from the ground. "Looks like you have her well in hand, Animal. I'll go see about using the sat phone to call to Fetch to arrange a pickup tomorrow."

After she left them alone, Allie leaned against the tree, all her energy leaving her body. "God, I'm tired."

"Well, you aren't getting much sleep tonight."

She raised her eyebrows. "Why's that?"

"Because you might have a concussion."

"I don't think I hit my head that hard."

"You thought you were shot. And you already have a goose egg on the side of your head."

Her shoulders fell. "How the hell am I going to stay awake?"

"Guess I'll have to keep you company. You like marshmallows?"

She blinked at his sudden segue. "I suppose."

"Well, you either do or you don't."

Irritated now, she frowned, which pulled on the bandage and made the wound sting. "Okay, I do." And because she wanted to annoy him right back, she asked, "Why are you called Animal?"

His eyes shuttered. But then he drew a deep breath. "I earned the name during my first mission in Iraq."

Allie nodded and softened her tone. "That's right. Carly told me you were a SEAL."

He blew out a breath that filled his cheeks. His glance slid toward the camp, which was swarming with people doing things. "We were pinned down in a firefight. Outmanned. Only way out was down a narrow alley. Insurgents on both ends. We flipped a coin to decide which direction we'd go. We knew we were toast, but we weren't waiting until we were out of bullets for them to storm right through us. We were going out with a fight."

Allie held her breath as he spoke, not wanting to distract him from finishing. His expression was hard to read—not particularly tense, just telling the story as though he was an observer, not someone who'd lived through the incident.

"We were tossing around ideas, the best way to take out as many as we could before we went down. I got pissed, thinking about the fact the bastards would be picking us off like ducks in one of those carney games. I grabbed my rifle, started roaring, and ran for the end of the alley, shooting at the walls, the windows, the men poking their heads around the corners.

"I must have looked like a lunatic, because I scared them. They bolted. We made it out without losing a man."

"Like you charging that bear..."

"Yeah, I guess," he said, his mouth curving at the corners.

Remembering what Carly had said about him, Allie pressed her lips together then wrinkled her nose. "I can't believe you told me that story. I didn't think you were much of a talker."

"I'm not." He shook his head and scowled down at her.

"Right. It's just me, then?"

"Guess so."

So, he was back to short answers. That was okay with her. She'd enjoyed listening to his rumbling voice as he'd told his story and liked the way he'd betrayed how much he'd cared about the men he'd served with. He'd been willing to sacrifice himself and had provided a distraction to help them escape. His howls had no doubt come straight from his soul at the thought of losing them.

She'd witnessed firsthand what that looked and sounded like.

"You hungry?" he asked.

She shook her head then gave him a tentative smile. "Maybe some of those marshmallows you mentioned..."

He moved away, leaving her propped against the tree she'd brained herself on.

Around the camp, the team was busy adding more branches to the fire, rolling out sleeping bags, and securing prisoners to trees, well apart from each other.

She raised her camera and begin clicking.

ANIMAL WALKED a little way into the woods. They'd think he was relieving himself, but he needed a little time to get himself together. When Allie had squealed in his ear, letting them all know she was nearby, his stomach had clenched. The moment Tibbets had drawn on Allie, he'd seen red—a damn wave of it clouding and narrowing his vision. He'd been ready to tear the man's head off, but he'd been forced to hold still, to watch as Tibbets mocked them, his gaze never leaving Allie, his finger sliding on the trigger of his gun.

When she'd pitched sideways, he'd launched himself at Tibbets, but the bastard squeezed off a shot, and Allie cried out.

After tossing away Tibbets's gun, he'd given him several hard punches, but then Reaper was there, and he'd torn himself away and run straight to Allie. For a second, his hand had shaken as he'd reached to touch the thick moisture on the side of her head. Once again, his heart had thudded like a bass drum, but then he'd noted the wound was shallow. And he remembered that she'd cried out half a second *after* Tibbets had fired.

His relief had been so great he'd nearly laughed, but then he'd seen how scared she'd looked. She'd knocked herself silly and thought she'd been shot. Only the fact that people were crowding around them kept him from pulling her into his arms.

An urge that confounded him. Sure, he'd love to get her into bed, now that he'd spent some time near her, learned her curves, her smell. What man wouldn't? But wanting to comfort her? That hinted he was falling a little deeper into infatuation than he ought to allow.

So, here he was, standing alone in the moonlight trying to pull himself together. He heard footsteps approach, so he quickly unzipped and began to piss.

"Think she might be concussed?" Reaper asked, giving him some space.

"Doubt it," he mumbled. "Still, someone should keep an eye on her. Try to keep her awake for a while."

"That someone you?"

Animal tucked and zipped, then turned to Reaper. "Someone else want the job?"

One side of Reaper's mouth curved. "We've already assigned shifts to keep eyes on the prisoners. Carly left you out of the rotation. Be warned. I think she's matchmaking."

Animal grunted. "I'll keep an eye on her. But Carly's going to be disappointed."

Reaper nodded. "Yeah, but it might be a good idea to pretend interest, so she won't throw random women in your path."

Animal shook his head. "Seriously, your woman does that?"

"Women, plural. Every one of the girlfriends and wives are so damn happy, they think it's their duty to spread it around."

"That works?"

"Has so far," Reaper drawled.

"Shit."

Reaper patted his shoulder. "You'll get used to 'em."

Animal cleared his throat. "I better head back to Allie and get her settled for the night." He frowned as he walked away, but he wasn't truly irritated over the fact Carly was trying to set him up with Allie. Seemed like a strange damn way to hook up a friend. Not like a blind date in a restaurant. No, Carly would make sure he tended to an injured woman in the middle of nowhere. He couldn't exactly wine and dine her. And since when was that even something he wanted to do?

He rubbed a hand over his face. Damn, his beard was kind of scruffy. Why on earth would a woman like Allie even look at him as something other than a photo-ready moment?

Back at the camp, he pulled out his sleeping bag and unrolled it on the ground near enough to the fire for warmth but far enough away to avoid pesky embers flying out to singe. He also dug out the bag of marshmallows. Then he moved to Allie whose eyes were closed as she slumped against the tree. He knelt beside her, lifted her into his arms, and stood.

Her eyes blinked slowly open. "I can walk, you know," she said, her tone dry.

"Figured I'd save your feet for tomorrow's hike."

She grimaced. "Three days more walking?"

"Naw. We're cutting straight west until we hit the highway. We have folks who'll pick us up there."

"One day...two?"

"If we get an early enough start, we'll be there early afternoon."

She glanced around them. "Are you planning on holding me all night?"

That didn't sound like such a bad idea. A few less clothes would be ideal, but they did have an audience.

"Why are you looking at me like that?" she whispered.

He didn't answer. If he told her he wished he could carry her deeper into the woods to fuck her, he'd probably lose her trust. No, *definitely*. She was hurt. He wasn't a bastard.

He strode toward the bed roll he'd prepared and set her down on top of it.

"I left my sleeping bag back in the meadow," she said. "I only brought a mylar blanket. This isn't mine."

"It's mine," he bit out.

"Oh." Her gaze fell away. "If we opened it, we could use my blanket to keep off the chill."

Was she proposing that they sleep together? "I can wrap up in your blanket. That was what you were planning to do, right?"

She nodded. "Still could."

"You're aching. The bag gives you a little padding."

He heard chuckling from across the fire and glanced toward Carly, who lay on her side, her head propped on a hand, watching them. He gave her a scowl, which only sent her into full laughter.

When he glanced back down at Allie, she was unzipping his bag and laying it open.

"See? Plenty of room. Didn't realize they made them this long." Then her gaze moved up his body. Had she paused when she'd swept past his crotch? Unbidden, his groin tightened.

Hook walked into the clearing and dumped her yellow backpack beside them. "Went back to where she was *supposed* to wait. Thought she might need it."

Animal opened her pack, drew out her blanket, and tossed it at Allie. She stood and unwrapped her blanket then shook it out with a crack before letting it settle over the sleeping bag. Their bed was made.

"I'll go find us sticks to roast those marshmallows," he said, knowing he sounded like he was gargling marbles, and then turned on his heel to disappear into the forest, again.

CHAPTER 5

FOR WHAT FELT like the twentieth time that night, Animal gently shook Allie awake.

She woke not feeling any disorientation. She'd fallen asleep with her head resting on his beefy arm, inches between their bodies, and she'd awoken with his body spooned around hers.

She kept her breathing even and deep, not wanting to alert him to the fact she was fully awake. Then she gave into the temptation of resettling against him, leaning harder on his chest, pushing her ass into his groin.

Lord, she hadn't dreamed that either. Animal's cock was erect. She wished she faced him, because she imagined herself brave enough to cup him in both hands to measure his length and tease him. Of course, she'd pretend to still be sleeping. A girl couldn't be held responsible for what happened when she was drifting along in a sexy dream.

She wriggled again, rubbing a little harder, and felt his cock jerk.

"Do that again," he whispered in her ear, "and I won't care how many people are sleeping around us."

"Not awake," she said, smiling with her eyes closed.

His grunt jerked his belly against her back. "You know the drill."

She groaned and rolled to her back.

A light flicked on, and he held it high and quickly flashed it across her eyes. "Still have a headache?"

"No. Told you the last time, I'm fine." She squinched her nose. "But I have to pee."

"I'll go with you."

She rolled her eyes. "You will not."

"You might run into another bear. I'm going."

"Do you think you're whispering?" Hook growled. "For fuck sake, go pee. And you might as well give up, Allie. He's not letting you go alone. I wouldn't either."

"Me either," Mace echoed.

She hit Animal's chest with her open palm and glared at him.

His smile made her heart flutter. It was filled with masculine satisfaction.

Allie tossed back the blanket and pushed up from the ground. When she stood, she raised her arms high to stretch.

She felt cool air brush her bare belly and quickly

pulled down the hem of the tank she wore beneath her open plaid shirt.

When she glanced at Animal, he was sliding his pistol into his holster. Then he flicked the end of his flashlight and pointed it toward the woods.

She preceded him, letting him aim his light around her as they walked away from the camp.

"How far you planning to go?" he drawled.

"I don't want them to hear."

"Darlin', everybody pees."

"Well, I'm not used to having an audience listen while I do it." Finally, she halted, glanced around, then cocked her ear toward the direction of the camp. She didn't hear any sounds coming from that direction and deemed this place perfect. "Now, walk away," she said, waving her hand at Animal.

He huffed. "I'm not going anywhere. A bear or a cougar could jump out of the bushes and drag you away."

She crossed her arms over her chest. "I am not going while you're standing right there." When he continued to give her that stone-faced look that passed for his version of patience, she walked several steps farther away.

She glanced over her shoulder. "You can at least turn around."

He turned sideways. "This is as much privacy as I'm giving you. We also don't know whether any more of the Tibbets clan are combing the forest, looking for their boys."

Keeping her gaze on him, she buttoned the bottom of her plaid shirt to close it, then reached beneath it to open her jeans and push them down. Everything was hidden. When she squatted, she held still for several seconds then groaned. It wasn't happening.

That was when she heard a zipper scraping.

She darted a glance at Animal and watched as he opened his jeans and pulled out his penis. "Um, what are you doing?"

"Thought you might be a little shy. I'm helping," he said, his tone dry as dust. Then he gripped his penis, aimed, and released his stream.

Interestingly, her own quickly followed.

How mortifying was this? And exciting. And funny. When she was done, she pulled a small wad of toilet paper from her pocket and wiped.

She didn't dare keep watching as Animal shook himself and tucked away his, uh...*member*. Okay, so she'd watched him pee. She'd seen his penis. And even only a little aroused, he was big. When she straightened and finished righting her clothes, he strode toward her and held out a small bottle of hand sanitizer. She opened her palm and let him give her a squirt.

The moment felt intimate. Charged. Her nipples prickled, and it wasn't from the chill in the air.

"We should get back," he said, his voice a quiet rasp.

"I'm not tired," she said, rubbing her arms. "It'll

be hard not making a bunch of noise moving around under that crackly blanket."

"Mace and Taco finished off the marshmallows."

"I'm not hungry."

Animal's chest rose.

Was he irritated she wasn't falling in line? "Sorry. You must be pretty tired, having to put up with me."

"I'm not tired."

The ragged edge of his voice caught her attention. Slowly, she raised her head so she looked up into his face, which was only partly visible in the moonlight. His eyes glittered. "What are you, then?"

"Horny."

Her mouth stretched. "Me, too."

He grimaced and readjusted his cock inside his jeans.

"Well, what do you think we ought to do about it?"

He shook his head. "We should head back."

"I won't sleep."

"Count sheep."

"I'm not used to sleeping with a man."

Animal drew another deep breath and reached out to tuck a lock of her hair behind her ear. "What the hell do you want with me, Allie? I would've thought a woman like you could have your pick of men."

"A woman like me?" she said, lowering her eyebrows. When he didn't explain, she turned on her heel and stepped out.

Animal snaked an arm around her waist and brought her back against his front. "Maybe that didn't come out right. I meant...a pretty woman like you."

Lord, she wanted to rub on him. Wanted to reach back and pull his beard to bring his mouth down to her neck. Fucking would be easy. Pants partway down, her bent forward, gripping a tree trunk.

He smoothed his hand over her belly then slipped it under her two shirts and pressed against her skin. She felt the pressure in her womb and arched her back to rub her ass against him. She couldn't stand it—being this close and not answering the call to nature she'd really been following when she'd led him away from camp.

Reaching past his hand, she unbuttoned the bottom of her shirt and spread the edges. Then she tugged the tank and shoved it upward, past her bra. Lastly, she opened the front clasp of her bra. With her breasts exposed to the cool air, her nipples tightened. She pushed out her chest, inviting him to touch it, hoping he'd look over her shoulder to see.

His hands moved slowly, rising past her ribs, palms turning to cup the undersides of her breasts. The first stroke of a callused thumb across a tip released fluid between her legs. "I'm wet," she gasped.

Behind her, he groaned. "I don't have a condom."

"Doesn't matter," she said, "touch me."

His hands squeezed her breasts, massaging,

pulling. When he thumbed the tips again, she quivered against him.

He gripped her waist and quickly turned her. Kneeling in front of her, he tugged her jeans farther down her thighs. For a few long seconds, he stared at her breasts and her pussy.

She wished she was nude and that she could straddle that thick thigh he leaned on. She'd never felt like this. Raw, charged, desperate.

When his gaze rose to meet hers, she read the question there. Was she sure?

In answer, she reached out and thrust her fingers deep into his warm, wild hair and bent toward him. The moment her mouth touched his, she moaned and opened. His tongue swept inside, mating with hers.

Then his hands were on her hips, her ass, slipping between her legs.

Awkwardly, without breaking the kiss, she toed off her boots and stepped on her jeans until she freed one leg, and then she lowered her body to that thick thigh to grind her pussy on it, and she pressed her chest against his, letting his hair tangle around her sharp tips.

His hands cupped her ass and squeezed. "I want to fuck you," he whispered, his face rubbing against her neck.

"You can. Take out your cock."

"No condom."

"I'm wet. We can rub against each other. It'll be enough. Swear."

He lifted her off his thigh and knelt on both knees while he opened his pants. The second he freed his cock, he groaned and fisted it. "Thought it was gonna strangle in my jeans." Then he reached for her.

Allie straddled him, teasing him with swirls of her wet pussy against the crown. He latched his mouth around a nipple and sucked it, drawing so hard she felt the tug all the way to her curling toes. "Yes," she gasped. "This one, too," she said, pushing her tits together so that he could lap at both with a slight turn of his head.

While she held her breasts for him to suck, he guided her hips downward, letting his cock nudge against her opening then sliding it away. When she settled against him, his cock glided through her folds.

He bit her nipple, and she let loose a breathy laugh. "Again!"

While he tugged and chewed, she rolled her hips, encouraging him to drive his cock through her folds, mimicking fucking. But it wasn't enough for her or him. She knew. His body vibrated with tension.

She raised a palm to her mouth and licked it. Then she curved her hand around the exposed side of his thick cock to give him the sensation of being surrounded. Now, he began to move in earnest. Rubbing against her. Building friction. Holy fuck, he was strong, moving her, controlling her. For a second, she contemplated begging him to come into her, because she wanted to feel all that power thrusting inside. "I'm close."

He lowered a hand and captured the head of his cock, then he directed it to rub against her clit as he moved, rocking against her body. Fingers tucked into the crease of her ass; one digit pushed against her ring. She jerked against him, staring down at him, her eyelids dipping, her mouth sagging open as he pushed again and slipped inside. She bit her lower lip to hold back a cry and exploded.

As they rubbed together, their movements more frantic, she felt his release wet her belly and hand. When they slowed, she slumped against him and wrapped her arms around his shoulders. With his face tucked into the corner of her shoulder, she combed his hair with her fingers, soothing him, calming herself.

"That was..." She shivered hard.

His arms surrounded her, hugging her closer.

"You okay?" he asked, his voice a little ragged.

"Never better," she murmured. And she realized she spoke the truth. Even though he hadn't penetrated her, she'd never come so hard. When he drew back his head, she kissed him again.

He cradled her face in his hands. "Think you'll sleep now?"

She smiled against his mouth. "Just try to wake me in the morning."

His mouth slid into a sexy, smirk.

"Yeah, be proud. You earned it," she said, jogging her eyebrows up and down.

Without letting her rise, Animal pulled off his

shirt. Then he used it to wipe up the mess he'd made all over her belly and hand.

"Think they'll know?" she whispered.

"Yeah. Do you care?"

She shook her head. "Hell, no."

He held her chin and kissed her. When they broke away, he gripped her waist and guided her upward. Then he held her jeans while she shoved her foot inside the leg she'd freed and pulled her jeans and undies upward, pausing to clean her pussy.

"I can do that," she said, reaching down for his shirt.

But he shoved away her hand and continued to clean her folds. When he'd finished, he bent toward her clit and sucked it.

"Ah," she said, her head falling back.

"Another time," he murmured. "I promise."

"I'll hold you to that. Next time, condoms."

"A fucking box of them," he growled.

After they dressed each other, he held her hand as he led her back to the camp.

All was quiet, but she knew it was ruse. The team was being polite. They settled on the sleeping bag and covered their bodies with the blanket. Then Animal pulled her close against his chest.

She drifted away into sleep held within his arms, and she knew she'd never felt so content.

At dawn, Animal rolled over her body and came up on his arms.

She stirred, a smile curving her mouth before she opened her eyes. He'd never seen anything so beautiful.

"Camp's stirring," he whispered as he ducked down to kiss her mouth.

"Oh!" Her eyes opened wide.

"Regrets?" he said softly, holding still for her answer.

"Not one. But you're on top of me...and we're not alone..." she said, lowering her brows.

He grunted as he gave her a nod. Then he moved to the side, climbed to his feet, and held out his hand to help her stand.

He knew from the secret smiles on the faces of those around them that everyone was aware of what had happened between them, but he didn't give a damn. He just hoped they wouldn't embarrass her with any teasing remarks. He aimed a glare around at the group as a warning but was met with chuckles.

Allie's cheeks were pink, but she seemed okay with the attention as she folded her blanket and returned it to her pack. Then she helped him roll up his sleeping bag. He tied the straps around it and attached the bag to his pack.

The team covered the fire with dirt, picked up trash, and then walked the prisoners one last time into the brush to relieve themselves.

At last, they began the long hike to the highway.

Animal took up the rear, just behind Allie. Every now and then she'd glance back at him. She didn't smile, but maybe she was trying to figure out what his expressions meant.

For his part, he was busy mulling over the many changes in his life that had occurred over the past few days.

He'd made his decision about the job. He liked the crew, and hunting was a natural fit. Where else could he use the skills he'd honed in the military? Law enforcement had been another option he'd pondered for a while, but he didn't like how restrictive the rules governing officers' conduct were. Yeah, he'd enjoyed wiping Tibbets's face in the dirt when he'd taken him down.

And he couldn't hide out on his mountain any longer, keeping away from people. He needed money to continue to his renovations.

The only open question for him now was whether Allie would want to see him again. Once they were back in civilization, would she decide he was a little outside her comfort zone? He rubbed his beard. He could clean up. Become more presentable —at least in appearance. But on the inside, he was still the same man. Still operating on primal conditioning. On instinct.

Still dangerous.

He'd slept lightly after they'd had sex, afraid he'd relax too much and that some old memory would rise up to shatter his peace. Maybe it was time to take the advice of the shrink he'd visited before he'd mustered out. Maybe he needed a therapist to work through some of the issues he carried around inside him. But all of that would take time. Right now, he felt an urgency to get Allie to commit to see him. They had unfinished business that would require an entire box of condoms.

CHAPTER 6

A FEW DAYS LATER, Animal entered the agency's office. It was early morning. A light shone in the kitchen just off the bullpen. He followed the aroma of fresh coffee.

Brian saw him enter and held up the carafe. "Shall I pour a cup?"

"Please."

"Need me to run you through access to the system again?" Brian asked as he filled two cups.

"No. I think I've got it."

He handed Animal a cup then rolled his chair to the table. "So, why are you here so early?"

Animal shrugged. "Just feeling restless."

Brian nodded. "I can imagine after going on a major hunt, like the one for Tibbets, that catching tweakers who miss their drug tests has to be a bit of a letdown."

Animal chuckled. "Yeah. I'm not good with downtime."

"You guys are all adrenaline junkies," Brian said smiling. "You'd like all our bailjumpers to be big bad dudes with huge bonds. Doesn't always work that way."

Animal sipped his coffee. "I like a paycheck as much as everyone else. A bigger payday would be nice, but that doesn't mean I won't take an afternoon to round up someone who needs to blow on a breathalyzer."

"Well, like I told you on day one, hunters tend to check our skips database, look for who is bumping up against the deadline for them to appear before their bail is forfeited to the court. Urgency is one determination —but so is the size of the bond. I'm trying to scrub the list to look out farther than a couple of weeks for the bigger fish, someone we have to scramble a team for."

"Like Tibbets."

"Yeah. Fetch likes that we're able to scramble and react quickly when needed, but he'd like to figure out ways to plan for ops, too. He's wanting to branch out a bit, loan out hunters to law enforcement, for instance."

Animal arched an eyebrow. "To help on a manhunt? He did mention we roll out when rewards are offered for apprehensions."

"Yeah, but also for missing persons searches, boots on the ground kinds of investigations."

"That would certainly keep things from getting boring around here."

Brian's gaze narrowed as he studied Animal's face. "Heard you and that photographer were pretty chummy."

Animal gave him a scowl.

Brian grinned and held up his hands. "I'm not judging. Heard she was hot."

Animal cleared his throat. "We have a date on Friday—if I'm not in the field."

"Ah." Brian chuckled. "You want me to make sure your schedule is clear...?"

"Nah," Animal said, then let a grin stretch his mouth. "I'm the new guy. I can't ask for favors."

The front door chime sounded. A moment later, Lacey and Dagger sailed into the kitchen. Lacey slid a bakery box filled with pastries onto the table. "Anyone want doughnuts?" She grabbed a napkin from the dispenser then opened the box and plucked a huge apple fritter from the assortment.

Animal shook his head. "How do you keep your figure?"

Lacey arched a brow. "Plenty of exercise."

Dagger patted her ass. "I let her do all the work."

Brian laughed.

Animal ducked his head and sipped his coffee. He liked how freely everyone in the office, save for Brian, talked about their sex lives. Nothing tawdry, but it seemed like everyone was getting some.

"Animal wants to make sure his schedule's free Friday night," Brian drawled.

Animal cleared his throat and aimed a glare at Brian.

"Oh?" Lacey settled in the chair beside him. "Does Friday have anything to do with the fact your photographer friend will be in town?"

Animal didn't have the heart to try to intimidate Lacey into dropping her line of questioning. Her open expression was kind of irresistible. He could see why Dagger followed her around to keep her out of trouble, although Reaper had warned him that Lacey was likely the smartest person in the office. He'd been told to never underestimate her ability to get what she wanted. A quality Reaper seemed to admire. "Uh, maybe."

"I knew it! You're going on a date, aren't you?"

Animal sighed. "Not sure it's a date. Don't even know how to date. It's been a while."

"Well, you've come to the right person—"

"I wasn't asking for advice," he said, shaking his head.

Dagger stood behind Lacey busting a gut trying to not to laugh out loud.

Brian's eyes teared up, and his shoulders shook. "Just give up. Lacey's on the job."

She reached out toward his hair. "Do you mind?"

Animal arched a brow but didn't duck away when she combed through his hair, tugging it this way and that.

"You need a trim."

He thought he needed a buzzcut. His hair hadn't been this long when he'd been a SEAL and long hair and a beard had been helpful blending into a Middle Eastern crowd.

"I can do it," she said, digging into her huge glittery tote bag. She pulled out scissors.

"Now?" he said, growing alarmed.

"Promise I've got mad skills. I do everyone's hair."

"Now, aren't you glad you came in early?" Brian said, backing up his chair and wheeling himself out the door.

Dagger glanced at Animal. "You're in good hands. But if she asks if you want mousse—say no." He turned and left too.

She scrunched her nose. "Just because it smelled like roses..." she sang after him.

"Took a damn week to wash out," he called out.

Lacey stood. "You better lose the shirt. I don't have a cape." She moved to the cupboard to rifle through a drawer and pulled out a tablecloth and clip. "This'll do."

"Look, you don't have to go to all this bother," he said, feeling his cheeks begin to heat.

Lacey cupped his face and locked her gaze with his. "Now, Animal, do you want Allie ready to climb you like a tree?"

He swallowed. The imagery was enticing.

"Trust me," she said, her blue eyes stretching as

she smiled. "I won't use the rose-petal mousse. And for your information, I was testing out a product for one of my podcasts. *He volunteered.* I got an amazing number of likes. For some reason, women love to see big alpha guys who are willing to help out their girlfriends. And I'll cut your hair in stages. You can tell me when I've gone far enough. Now, the shirt—lose it."

He sighed and rose. When he removed his shirt, he ignored her low whistle.

"I heard that," Dagger shouted from the bullpen.

"I can look, baby." She smiled up at Animal. "I can see what she likes about you." Then she snapped her scissors closed and pointed toward the chair. "Sit."

Animal did so, bemused that she so easily directed his actions. Reaper was right. The woman was dangerous.

On Thursday, Allie parked her 4Runner in the MBH parking lot. She rather liked how quaint their building was with its clapboard siding and wraparound porch. No one looking at the exterior would imagine the roughhewn and muscly crew who worked there.

She glanced into her rearview mirror and checked her makeup. She didn't know why she'd bothered. She rarely wore any. She'd used a light hand that morning, not wanting to look like she was trying too hard.

No one expected her today. She'd scheduled a meeting for the next day with the team she'd observed and photographed. She needed releases signed and wanted to show them the shots she was considering submitting along with her writeup. As well, she had video she wanted to share with them.

And then there was her date tomorrow night with Animal. Or at least, she thought it was a date. Maybe it was just an invitation for a fuckfest. Before he'd handed her into the SUV that took her back to her vehicle in the park, he'd asked to see her when she returned to Bear Lodge, whatever that meant.

She'd brought an outfit to wear if they went to dinner and sexy lingerie if they headed straight to a hotel. After they'd been met on the highway with transports for the team and the Tibbets cousins, she'd realized that one of the vehicles was there expressly for her. She'd glanced around to find Animal loading his pack into another vehicle.

He'd frowned and approached her, but they'd had an audience, and again, he was gruffly direct when he'd spoken. "When will you be in Bear Lodge?"

"Friday, I think," she'd said, feeling breathless and little unmoored. Her mind had been filled with this man for the past two days. The thought that they were about to be separated had made her feel anxious.

He'd reached for her hand and tugged her body closer. Leaning toward her, he'd looked into her eyes. "Friday."

She'd nodded, reading into his hard stare that he planned to pick up where they'd left off in the early morning hours. But maybe she was reading more into that one word than he'd intended.

Now, she was having second, third, and fourth thoughts about her early arrival. She really should have waited to come, but over the last days, she'd been unable to concentrate. Sleep was impossible. Every time she lay down, memories of what had happened between her and Animal flooded her mind. She'd refused to dig her vibrator out from under her bathroom sink. Only the real thing would do. She only hoped he didn't feel like she was stalking him, pushing too hard. Men tended to like to do the chasing, or so she'd read in Cosmo.

Taking a deep breath, she grabbed her camera bag and the big brown envelope, holding copies of her photos and a thumb drive, and stepped out of her vehicle.

Entering the office, she heard the doorbell chime and glanced around. She walked to the long polished counter that separated the lobby from a group of desks. The place appeared deserted, until she heard a whirring sound. She watched as a man in a wheelchair rolled toward the low counter.

He was dark-haired and handsome. A tug of regret filled her noting the missing legs. Because he worked for Montana Bounty Hunters, she felt safe assuming he was ex-military.

His gaze met hers, taking in her face and the camera case hanging from her shoulder. "Allie Travers, right?" he said, smiling.

She smiled back. "Yes. I am. And you must be the Brian I spoke to on the phone."

He gave her a nod and pointed toward the end of the counter. "Come on around." When she moved around it, he backed up his chair and led her deeper into the office. "I just made a fresh pot of coffee. It's late in the day, so I expect the hunters to start straggling in."

Inside a small kitchen area, he waved a hand toward the table then moved to the Bunn coffee pot on the counter. He wrinkled his nose as he picked up the glass carafe. "I like it strong."

"So do I—and black."

"Then you're in luck. I ran out of creamer. Lacey used the last."

She didn't know who Lacey was, but she smiled when he brought her cup.

Once he placed his on the table in front of him, he clasped his hands. There was humor in his gaze as, again, he scanned her face.

Embarrassed, she made a face. "Did I not blend my makeup well? I don't wear it often."

He chuckled. "No, you're prettier than I thought you'd be." Then he laughed and shook his head.

"That came out wrong. What I meant was, I had this idea that you were this Amazon woman—big shoulders, tall—because you spend time out in the wilderness all on your own. I figured you'd look like someone who could wrestle a cougar or a bear." When he finished, he raised his eyebrows. "I hope I didn't offend you."

Instantly, Allie decided she liked Brian Cobb. "You didn't offend me. And I wish I was that Amazon. I'm having a bit of a crisis of confidence after what happened out there."

"Because Animal rescued you from the bear?"

She nodded and sipped her cup. "Guess you heard all about it."

"I hear everything. Sometimes, more than I want to hear, but these bounty hunters are a gossipy group."

"Even Animal?"

Brian shook his head. "He's still new. I have faith though that the women will get to him."

"Women?"

"Oh, don't worry. Every woman here is spoken for."

"I wasn't worried..." When he arched a brow, she blushed.

His dark eyebrows waggled. "Not sure how long he'll be. For the past couple of days, he's been trying to bring in a shoplifter." Brian laughed and dumped a packet of sugar into his coffee. "He didn't need a warrant to enter her house, but her husband was telling the truth when he said she wasn't there. Now, he's pretty sure she's hiding out in her mama's house. We don't have the legal right to just walk in there, and Mama refused to let Animal inside, so he's been staking out the house, waiting for her to leave."

Allie shook her head. "She failed to show for a trial for shoplifting? What's she going to get, a fine?"

"She knows the judge. They dated in high school. She's convinced he's going to make her sit in jail because she dumped him after the prom."

"Well, if he has to wait for her to move, couldn't that go on a while?"

Brian grimaced. "I suppose, but then Myra would miss Thursday night bingo."

Another smile tugged at her mouth. "He's waiting for her to sneak out to play bingo?"

With his expression solemn, Brian nodded. "People take their bingo seriously around these parts." He gave her a wink. "You know, it starts around five. Serious players get there early to set up their cards."

Allie pushed up from her seat. "Where's this bingo parlor?"

Ten minutes later, she found a parking space on Main Street, across the street and a couple of storefronts down from the game hall with the big neon "Bingo" sign in the window.

Brian had promised to ping her phone if Animal

caught Myra slipping out of her mother's house. He'd also described Animal's beat-up pickup—which she spotted several parking spaces in front of hers. Warmth filled her just looking through the back window of his truck at his big head and shoulders, although something about his silhouette had changed.

It was the hair. It didn't seem "big" enough.

Brian had also shared a picture of Myra Brown, so she watched the people heading into the parlor, but didn't see anyone who fit the description of the too-red-to-be-a-real-redhead whose license said she was born in 1952 and was five-foot-four and a hundred-fifty pounds, but whose photo made one wonder if she'd shaved fifty pounds off her official weight.

Allie liked this, sitting near him, waiting with him. She reached for her camera and took a few shots through her windshield. Seemed she was always looking at the world through her lens. She twisted the lens to zoom in, just in time to see him turn his head. He was frowning. God, she loved that expression, because his dark brows were thick and gave him a slightly menacing look, and his narrowed eyes made her heart skip a beat.

He didn't really frighten her, but she liked the hint of danger that surrounded him. She'd felt how powerful his body was and had seen how fast he could move for such a big man. Damn, she wanted more of that.

His mouth curved, and he opened the truck's door.

She glanced toward the sidewalk across the street and noted a woman wearing a baggy sweatshirt and what looked to be a bad wig, because the brown hair was a solid toffee color and stood out around her head. Allie took more shots, gleeful she was capturing the moment.

She couldn't make out much about the woman's features because she wore oversized sunglasses. Her lips were pinched into a flat line, and she was walking too fast, like she was trying to be nonchalant and too afraid to run.

Animal quickly crossed the street, intercepting the woman before she could duck inside the bingo parlor door. "Myra Brown, I'm a Fugitive Recovery Agent. I'm taking you to jail." He held out his hand to show the badge he cupped then reached for her elbow.

But she backed away and screamed, "Help me! I'm being assaulted. Help me!"

Allie's eyes widened, and she jerked open her door. As she jogged toward them, people swarmed out of the parlor.

Animal held up his badge. "Now, folks, there's no need to be concerned. I'm a bounty hunter, and Myra, here, skipped her court date."

It appeared Myra's friends didn't care that she'd broken the law and was a fugitive. They flooded around the two, cutting off Animal from Myra, who continued to back away then turned and fled.

Cursing, Animal tried to wade through the geriatric crowd but wasn't making any progress.

Allie stared after Myra and then made up her mind. No way was Animal going to waste another day looking for the woman. She ran after Myra who already had a half-block advantage.

"Allie, what the hell are you doing?" Animal called after her.

"Catching your skip!" she shouted over her shoulder.

Myra moved fast for a woman her size and age. She had just reached her old Buick and was angling her body to slide behind the wheel, when Allie caught up with her. "Ma'am, I can't let you escape."

"Mind your own business," Myra groused, settling heavily in her seat. "You gotta badge? You don't have a badge, I'm not your business!"

Allie blinked at the woman's raspy voice. "My boyfriend's business is my business. You're not going anywhere."

A throat cleared behind her, and she turned to find Animal standing there. The corners of his eyes were wrinkled like he was laughing, but his mouth was set in a straight line. "Lock your car up, Myra. You can have your husband pick it up later. Right now, you're going to jail."

WHILE ALLIE WAITED in Animal's truck as he took Myra inside the jail for booking, she reviewed the pictures she'd taken. Myra's wig was askew as Animal held her arm to escort her inside. Her eyes were like black buttons in her wrinkled face, her mouth snarling in every shot.

Myra Brown was one mean lady. She wondered what her parents looked like.

Allie chuckled as she came to the picture of Animal being surrounded by so many white-haired and balding people. She hit a button and zoomed in, looking at his expression, which was partly exasperated, although the curve of his mouth indicated he saw the humor in his situation, too.

The door beside her opened. He stood in the opening and reached for her. She hastily set aside her camera as he pulled her toward him. His kiss was hard. His body crowded hers. She had to part her legs to let him in closer. When he pulled back, his gaze was on her mouth. "Hope you wanted that, too."

All she could manage was a nod.

"Get your belt on," he said, then slammed shut her door and ran around the front of the truck to slip in beside her.

After a twist of his key, he hauled ass out of the detention center's parking lot.

Allie's breath caught watching him beside her. He'd cut his hair and trimmed his beard. She kind of missed the wild man, but his shaggy, chin-length hair was still long enough for her to comb with her fingers.

Something she couldn't wait to do. "Where are we going?"

"Damn." He frowned and darted a glance her way. "Didn't think. My place is kinda rough."

"Take me there," she blurted. She didn't care what it looked like so long as there was a bed.

Still frowning, he returned his attention to the road and smashed his boot against the gas pedal.

CHAPTER 7

SHE'D MISSED HIM. It was silly really. How many days had they been apart? Four? She ought to be alarmed over the fact she was obsessed with the rough man. They'd only spent two days in each other's company.

But he was unlike anyone she'd ever met, and he made her feel pretty wild and untamed herself. Brave enough to grab what she wanted. And what she wanted was him.

He turned off the highway and onto a graveled road. When he made another turn and changed gears to climb a steep trail, she wondered what was waiting at the top.

Dusk was gathering, but there was enough light to show a rather sad little cabin, sitting amid a chaos-strewn clearing, where logs lay in piles and equipment sat under tarps. He cut the engine. Only moonlight illuminated the area.

"It's a work in progress," he muttered, staring across at the cabin.

Did he think she was some prissy girl? Hadn't he met her on a mountain meadow facing down a bear? "Don't care. Do you have a mattress?"

His gaze cut to hers. In the scant, silver light she saw his mouth twitch. "Yes, ma'am."

She widened her eyes. "Well, get me there."

"Wait for me," he growled, then opened his door and walked around to open hers. He held out his hand. "Step where I step."

She chuckled. "That bad?"

"The flooring inside is...spotty. The old linoleum is gone, and I've been ripping out rotten plywood."

She took his hand and slid down from the truck. Then with her hand held inside his, she carefully picked her steps around logs, saws, and random tools, and climbed the uneven steps to the porch.

Once through the unlocked front door, he flicked on a flashlight and led the way through the house. Looking around, she noted the drywall had been removed and bare studs were exposed. Here and there were the holes in the flooring he'd mentioned. Down a short hallway, he opened a door. At least here, the plywood floor was complete and from the smell, new. A queen-size iron bed with a deep mattress stood in the center of the room. Again, the walls had been ripped out to expose wood framing.

"You did all this?" she said, glancing around.

"I've been demolishing." He flashed a light into a

darkened bathroom. "New fixtures inside there, and I've tiled the walls and floor."

"Priorities," she murmured.

"Yes. If I leave you here in the dark, do you promise not to move?"

She nodded.

"I'll be back in five." He hurried out of the room, leaving her in darkness, the sounds of his heavy foot-steps echoing through the house. A few minutes later, she heard the rev of an engine, and light flickered from a lamp sitting on a crooked nightstand next to the bed.

Her gaze went to the mattress. The bed was neatly made with an old-fashioned quilt covering it. Two fluffy pillows with green pillowcases. In one corner of the room rested an open duffel with clothing exploding from within.

He returned holding two water bottles. "They're room temperature," he said, handing her one.

Allie walked to the bed, twisted the top off her bottle, and sat on the edge of the mattress. She bounced once. No squeaks. Soft. Her gaze flitted back to him.

He stood still, as though waiting for something from her.

"You've done a lot of work," she said softly.

"I'm months away from making it livable. I work on it as I can. Now that I'm with the agency, I may not finish until early next year." He cleared his throat. "The power company's going to install poles in a couple of weeks."

She took a drink from her bottle and stared across at him. Then she set it on the nightstand and patted the bed beside her.

He swallowed hard and walked toward her. "I should have taken you to a hotel. I wasn't thinking. It's what I was going to do tomorrow night—after dinner—if you were willing."

"I kind of like the idea of being up on this hilltop in the middle of nowhere," she said softly. "Just you and me. It echoes in here," she said, her mouth curving into a smile.

"It does," her rasped.

She glanced at him from beneath her eyelashes. "Bet the wildlife will be able to hear us for miles."

Animal reached out for her hand and pulled her to her feet. He glanced down at her blouse. "The buttons are tiny," he said, frowning.

Smiling, she bent her head and began undoing them, one at a time.

When her blouse fell open, he pushed it off her shoulders and waited.

She unclasped her bra.

His hands rushed forward and cupped her breasts while she shrugged the garment away.

She toed off her boots and unbuttoned her jeans. The zip sounded loud—so did his breathing. When his hands slipped beneath the waistband to curve around her bottom, she drew a shaky breath.

Animal moved back a step and knelt. Then he pushed down her jeans while smoothing his hands over her legs, touching her everywhere. He nuzzled against her belly and nipped her, causing her to jerk and release a nervous laugh. When he shoved her jeans and panties to her ankles, she stepped out of them, one foot at a time to either side of her clothing, opening her legs. He laid his palm on her lower belly and pushed, forcing her to fall onto the mattress, then he lifted her legs and placed them on his shoulders and bent toward her pussy.

"So fast?" she bleated, reaching out for his hair to hold him back.

"Don't stop me," he said, his voice a deep, garbled rumble.

His tongue slid through her folds, moving from the bottom upward, stroking through them, pressing deep.

She fisted her hands in his hair to anchor him there, and arched her back, her breasts hardening, her belly quivering as he licked and probed, making little growling noises that vibrated against her tender flesh.

When he tunneled into her vagina, she felt a gush of fluid ooze from inside her, and he thumbed apart her folds to get closer, rubbing his cheeks and nose in her pussy, fingers toggling her clit, circling her anus. Thrilling alarm raced through her body. Goose bumps prickled her skin. She writhed on the bed, her hips undulating, while he explored her thoroughly.

Then he rose and stripped. Not teasing like a

strip show—it was a wild unveiling as he tossed away his clothes. When he straightened after shoving down his jeans, she gasped at the sight of his thick, heavily veined cock. Hers. Every inch.

He cloaked himself, rolling the condom down his length then gave himself a single, slow stroke, which she watched as though mesmerized.

With his eyelids lowering to slits, he moved toward her again and placed his thigh against her pussy. He crawled over her, scooting her with that hard, muscled thigh to the center of the mattress. Breathless now, she raised her knees and spread her thighs while stretching her arms above her head to grip the rungs of the iron bed. Showing him that she was his. Surrendering everything.

"You're so fucking beautiful," he said, his gaze roaming her pussy, her belly, her shivering breasts. Her nipples were dimpled, the tips sprung. When his fingers plucked them, she bit her lower lip and turned her head because the sensation was too much.

Animal thrust a hand under her ass, lifted her hips, then braced his weight with the other planted on the mattress beside her shoulder. With his hair falling forward, his gaze met hers for a long, charged moment.

"I haven't kissed you," he said, his thick eyebrows lowering.

She shook her head and glanced down at his cock. "Need," she whispered, her body trembling so hard he could see it.

He squeezed her ass then slipped the hand from under her to guide his cock to her pussy. He rubbed the tip in the moisture welling there, then ringed the base and flicked it at her open folds. It thudded, reminding her of its weight and girth. "I want to slap your cheek with my dick," he said, his narrowed gaze darting to hers.

She nodded. "Whatever," she whispered. Promising that anything he wanted she was willing to give.

"Hold back a bit, Allie. I want to stay a while inside you."

His whisper was a rough rasp that scraped along her skin. She let go of the rungs and molded her palms over his chest. She plucked his tiny nipples. "I'll try..."

When he nudged against her entrance, she arched her back and dug her head into the pillow, wanting to savor the way he entered her, pushing to breach her, then pulling back, easing deeper and deeper until she gloved every inch. His cock stretched her and seemed to expand even more when he held still. She dug her fingers into his shoulders. "Move," she whispered.

He gave her long, slow glides, his eyelids lowering and his nostrils flaring as he too seemed to savor the sensation of gliding through her slick channel.

She wrapped her arms around his back and scratched down his spine, her fingers dragging in the deep indention.

He went to his elbows and gave her shorter strokes, harder ones that jerked her hips and pushed the air from her lungs in winded gasps.

She didn't dare tilt her hips to let him rub against her clit or she'd be gone. Everything he did, every glide and thrust, built heat inside her. Sweat beaded on her forehead. Her nipples felt raw from rubbing against his chest hair. Too many sensations. She thrashed her head, trying to hold on.

But then he pulled free, abandoning her, and she clutched her own breasts as he moved to kneel between her legs.

"Turn around, Allie."

She blew a stream of air between her pursed lips and shook her head.

"Don't be afraid."

She started to scoff. Afraid? Her? She'd already been fucking him. What was there to fear? But then she realized she was. Without his face above hers, his gaze to anchor her, she would feel more vulnerable. And faced away, he controlled everything.

He fisted his cock, drawing her attention to it. Reminding her he had what she needed.

Giving him a frown, she moved slowly, because her body still trembled, and turned to face away. She came up on her knees.

He placed a hand in the center of her shoulders to hold her chest pinned to the mattress when she would have pushed up. "Like this," he said. Then he moved back.

Breath blew across her sex, and she buried her face in the bedding while he sucked at her folds and rimmed her entrance with his fingers. Then a fingertip touched her anus again, and she tightened. When his tongue glided over her there, she drew a sharp breath. "Oh, God!"

He didn't listen, swirling his tongue there, where no one had ever touched her. When a thick finger pushed on the ring, she was almost relieved, until it slipped inside—not just a fingertip—pushing deep then circling, easing her open.

She'd never imagined what that might be like. Never anticipated the pleasure. Soon, as he pumped and circled on her forbidden hole, she felt as though he'd drugged her, because her moans came freely, deepening as he resumed playing with her pussy, his tongue fluttering against her clit.

She'd thought he was wild man. Unrefined. That sex with him would be hard and fast and...basic. But this blew her mind. Her breaths grew more ragged, edging on sobs. She rubbed her breasts against the comforter, needing relief, needing him to take her.

When he removed his fingers and tongue, she was wrung out, pliant as she'd never been with another man. As his hands gripped the notches of her hips and his cock aligned with her pussy, the only movement she could make was to drop her belly so that her ass rose just a little higher. The rest was up to him because she was already boneless.

Or so she thought until he entered her and began to thrust. And not gently.

He pounded inside her, his grip bruising, his body hard and sweating behind her.

She shook her head and went to her elbows to brace against his thrusts, just high enough her nipples raked the fabric beneath her. Having been in a constant state of arousal, she was mindless, her hands bunched in the bedding, whimpers bursting from her when he quickened.

"Now, baby," he ground out. "Fucking fly with me!"

That's what her body had waited for. *Permission.* She threw back her head and screamed as pleasure exploded—everywhere. She couldn't have said where it started, just that it cramped her belly and curled her toes. Her pussy was juiced, so wet her ass and his belly smacked deliciously together, the slippery sounds echoing lewdly around them.

She keened as her orgasm unwound, and she hung in the moment, him jerking against her bottom, his hands cuddling her breasts. He kissed the top of her shoulder then rubbed his beard against her, rocking, supporting all her weight now, because she'd gone limp inside his embrace.

She roused when he brought her to the mattress and began to slide free. "No," she protested, reaching back to clamp her fingers on his ass. He pushed deep again, then inched them to their sides, where they lay spooned, chests heaving, sweat cooling on their skin.

Allie didn't know what to say. She'd never experienced anything like that before. Sex with him felt... like it was more than sex. For her, the earth had moved. She felt shattered.

How could she ever give this up?

He remained silent behind her, and she felt disappointment begin to creep in. "I need to clean up," she whispered.

His breath held. She felt his heart thud against her back. The hand on her breast tightened. "Don't leave."

She pushed against his hip and pulled away, and then slowly turned inside his embrace.

His expression was stark, his eyes... They locked on her face, and she knew he was feeling something of what she was feeling.

Relieved, she placed her palm against his cheek and stroked his lips with her thumb. "I didn't want to overstay."

He frowned. "We don't have to stay here."

She shook her head, smiling. "I don't care that your house is a construction site. I really don't." She paused and looked away, because she didn't want to scare him by letting him see everything she felt. "I was...a little overwhelmed."

"I won't do *that* again. If you hate it."

She kissed his mouth to shut him up. "I didn't say I hated anything. Animal..." She grabbed her courage and looked him in the eye. "Sex has never been that way for me. I've never trembled, never been left feeling completely wrung out. When I said I was overwhelmed, I should have said...I was amazed."

One corner of his mouth twitched. "If I tell you the truth, it won't scare you?"

She shook her head and braced herself inside.

"I wanted to overwhelm you. Didn't want you to breathe unless I let you." He swallowed.

"I've never been this...into a woman."

She drew a deep breath and felt her eyes begin to burn. *Good Lord, I am not going to cry.* To hide her reaction, she slipped her arms around him and hugged him. Animal cradled her in his arms.

"I'm not sure how this will work," he said after a few minutes.

"You seemed to know exactly how everything worked."

He snorted. "Us. You're way down in Helena."

"I live in an apartment that's more of a storage unit. I go there to wash my clothes in between jobs."

"Your jobs take you everywhere."

"I'm the one who approaches editors with ideas for stories and photo layouts. I can work anywhere, and I can determine my schedule."

"Your storage unit apartment—could you move your stuff here? I mean, when I get this place put back together."

"I've never renovated a house..." she said, again dropping her gaze. She didn't want to seem like she was being pushy. He might need those months of work to get his head around the idea of having her around.

"Me neither. I've been watching a bunch of YouTubes." He swallowed hard. "We could learn together. I might not be so quick to chop shit up."

She blinked and stared at his smile that seemed almost sheepish. "I'm in." She wrinkled her nose. "Are you sure? This is kind of quick."

"Allie..." he said, cupping both sides of her face to keep her from looking away. He cleared his throat. "When we finished just now, fucking, that is...did you feel as though you'd die if we never did it again?"

This time, the tears came quick. She had to blink them away. She nodded because her throat closed up.

"Well, there it is," he said, his voice deepening. "We're in this together."

HE WAS LATE for work but couldn't have cared less. Not with Allie's tits bouncing in his face.

He'd come awake gradually, like drifting through clouds, the only thought coalescing was that his cock had to be in heaven.

Close enough. Her clever mouth had coaxed him into an erection, and now she was taking advantage of the "amenities" their living arrangement would provide—namely one "big-ass cock" for her to use whenever she needed her plumbing "snaked".

Her words. He'd grinned and folded his hands

behind his head as she'd taken her sweet time seducing him. By the time she'd screwed slowly down his cock, he'd been gritting his teeth, trying to hold back, because he didn't want to come before she'd pleased herself. He'd decided it was his manly duty, always, seeing as how he'd talked her into moving into his crappy cabin.

Now, he smiled to himself as she watched her cheeks grow rosy and her eyelids dip. As she rose and fell, she got wetter and wetter. Her busy hands weren't caressing him anymore, they were twisting her own nipples, and by the look of her scrunched-up nose, he didn't have much longer to hold out.

She halted her movements and gave him a dazed look.

"Baby, need me to take over?" he asked, pitching his voice lower, because he knew that made her shiver.

Sure enough, she quivered, and her mouth pouted. She gave a quick nod and abandoned his cock, moving to his side.

She didn't lie down and open her arms. She knelt beside him, her gaze locked on him. It occurred to him that she was waiting his instructions. If she'd still been sitting on his cock, he would have blown right then and there.

Allie had a submissive streak, something he would nurture but never abuse. She likely wasn't even aware of it. Warmth spread through him. Something that felt like...tenderness. Damn, he was falling hard for the woman. Thank God, she seemed to be suffering the same fate.

He went to his knees beside her. "Baby, lie on your back. Like you did last night. Raise your knees and open yourself. I like to look."

Her cheeks reddened, but she did as he asked. When she was spread, he arranged her hands to cup the undersides of her tits. Then he squeezed her hands to encourage her to plump up her breasts.

"That something you like to see, too?" she asked, her voice husky.

"Yes, baby." He moved her feet higher on the mattress and pressed on her knees. "Don't ever be shy," he said. "I like looking at your pussy."

Her breath hissed between her teeth.

"Don't like that word? Want me to call it...cunt?"

Her nose wrinkled. "Which do you prefer?"

He smiled, thinking she was just about perfect for him. "Read a book a million years ago. It used the word...quim."

She chuckled. "Were you reading a Victorian romance?"

He waggled his eyebrows. "Victorian porn, I think."

"I don't care what you call it."

"Then I'll call it *mine.*"

She gave a nod, and her hands plumped her breasts again.

Deciding he'd better hurry before her arousal

started to fade, he lowered himself over her, bracing on his hands. "Allie, put my dick inside you."

"The things you say..." She licked her lips and reached for him, both hands gripping him and giving him a slow stroke. Damn, he couldn't wait until they were both cleared by a doctor, because he never wanted to wear a rubber again. The thought of being inside her wet heat, uncloaked, was driving him crazy.

Allie placed his cock against her entrance.

Maintaining space between them, he nudged her sex but didn't push inside. He waited until she met his gaze. "Watch me take you."

Then he glanced down their bodies and entered her.

With her hips tilted the way he'd intended, he watched her vulva sink and swell with each stroke. Moisture coated his length and even to his own eyes, he looked incredibly large disappearing inside her. "How do you take me?" he growled.

"There's no room when you're deep," she gasped as he sank again and again. "No place to hide. Oh, Animal, I'm almost there."

He understood what she said. He'd fucked women before, never wondering how they felt, doing his duty to please them, but never feeling a connection. Never truly sharing. Not like this. Dropping down against her skin, he wrapped his arms around her body. "Baby, hold on." Then with short, quickening strokes, he drove them both over the edge.

CHAPTER 8

SINCE ALLIE HAD LEFT her car parked on Main Street the night before, she had to accompany Animal when he finally rolled into work.

Fortunately, their "walk of shame" wasn't nearly the ordeal it could have been.

Carly did give her legs a glance and said, "Well, you're not bowlegged."

Reaper swatted his woman and told her to be polite, but Carly gave her a wink, telling her silently that she was happy for her.

Allie decided to let her think that her matchmaking had been the extra "sauce" that pushed them together. She'd never admit to a soul that she'd been hooked the instant Animal had chased after that bear. There was just something about a wild, unfettered man. And she hadn't told him yet, but he was growing out his hair.

Everyone was there, desk chairs pulled around the desk with the big monitor while Brian brought up a spreadsheet with a list of names. Allie moved closer and realized it was a list of skips, which included the amounts of their bonds, the dates the bonds came due, their homes of record, and a description of their infractions.

"We've got some drug and alcohol skips. All close. All easy. If we could clean the oldest off the list today, we can all meet up again this afternoon. Fetch will be here. Said he'll spring for pizza." His gaze went to Allie. "He wanted to see what you have."

Her eyes widened. "Hell, I left my envelope here."

His mouth stretched in to a wide grin. "Yeah, you should never leave a thumb drive lying around. I have no morals when there are files to be opened. I sent him a picture or two. He sounds excited."

She shook her head and gave him a woeful look. "The thumb drive was inside the envelope...and there I thought you were my friend." He blinked, looking dismayed, and she laughed. "I was going to show you what I had anyway. It's part of what I'd like to get waivered."

He wiped a hand across his brow. "Whew. Thought I'd broken the circle of trust." For the next twenty minutes, he handed out assignments to the team members who looked disgruntled at the low-earning skips.

"Don't look so down," Brian said. "We've got a big job I'll tell you about later."

Allie followed Animal outside, hating the thought of having to kill time until the afternoon meeting.

"Want to come?" he asked, slapping his folder against his hand.

She brightened immediately. "Yeah. Promise I won't interfere again," she said, crossing her heart.

He shook his head. "Just get in the truck."

Animal ended up letting Allie question Rylee Adams's boss at Hair Hype to find out when she was scheduled to come in to work. Her boss had eyed Allie's messy braid and asked her if she wanted high-lights as well as a cut.

When she stepped up into the truck, she lifted her braid. "Do you think I need highlights? She called my hair mousy."

His eyebrows lowered. "You don't need to change a damn thing."

The heat in his tone went a long way toward soothing her irritation. She turned sideways in the seat. "She'll be in at eleven. We've got twenty minutes."

Animal nodded and glanced out the window, apparently content to remain silent while they waited.

She frowned. "I don't think I'd be very good at this job."

"You got the information we needed," he murmured. "You did great."

"No, I'm talking about this part. The waiting."

His head swung back to her. "But you sit behind a camera—waiting for shit to happen."

Allie shrugged. "That's different. I'm constantly fiddling with it, checking the lighting, the settings..."

"And I'm busy watching my surroundings. Like that guy over there who's waiting on his wife." He pointed to a man in a sedan parked near the sidewalk leading into the salon. "He's checked his watch three times in the last five minutes."

"So? Maybe he hates waiting, too."

"No, he's irritated because he's waiting on her. Bet if he was waiting on one of his drinking buddies to kiss his wife goodbye before they head to the strip club, he'd be just fine."

"So, you're a people watcher?" She glanced around and realized there were a lot of people to watch along the lazy main street. "That a skill you honed while in the military?"

He nodded. "During deployments, we always had to be aware of our surroundings. Situational awareness can keep you alive."

Allie slid her arm along the top of the seat and fingered his hair. "Why did you leave the Navy?"

He drew a deep breath and turned his head to stare out his window. "There wasn't any reason left to stay."

She was only mildly disappointed he didn't

continue. She hadn't known him long enough to think he'd spill all his secrets, but after a moment, he began to speak again.

"We were in Syria. Advising Kurdish forces fighting ISIS," he said, then paused to clear his throat. "Mostly, they needed us to call in air strikes, but that didn't mean we didn't fight. We shared their camp. We had some downtime and were playing basketball with the Kurds." His gaze grew distant. "First round hit, I remember the sound, the heat. Flying. When I woke up, I stood and looked around. Everyone was dead. In pieces. I barely had a scratch."

His voice was so hoarse when he finished, she wished she could scoot closer and put her arms around him, but his expression closed, and he glanced out the window again. "That's our girl." He opened his door.

She drew a sharp breath and turned to watch as a young woman with a spiky purple bob exited her car and made her way toward the salon. Picking up her camera, Allie zoomed in on Rylee, noting her pale skin looked almost blue next to the purple hair.

Rylee's gaze whipped to Animal who strode directly toward her. Her eyes widened, and then she tossed her purse at him and ran down a side street away from him.

Animal jogged after her. His strides were longer. He didn't have to expend as much energy as the short-legged stylist. When he didn't seem particularly eager to catch her, and the distance down the road stretched, Allie scooted across the bench seat of his truck and started it up. She pulled out onto the road and caught up with them, driving into the empty left lane, and slowing beside Animal as she rolled down the window. "You just gonna wait for her to get tired?"

He grimaced. "She's tiny. I don't want to hurt her."

"Ahhh. You're sweet." Allie grinned and drove up beside Rylee. "You know he's just letting you get tired."

"I can't go to jail," Rylee gasped, pressing a hand against her side. "They'll test me there. And then the judge'll make me stay the rest of my sentence."

Allie nodded and checked the road ahead of her. Still empty. "Why don't you use that time to get cleaned up? Then you won't have to worry about this ever again."

She rolled her eyes. "Have you met my family?"

"Nope. Not from around here."

"Well, cleaning up will never be a family affair."

"Then move away," Allie said. "Start fresh."

Rylee gave her a scowl.

By this point, Rylee was only walking fast, and Animal looked like he was taking a stroll. "Oh, for Pete's sake," Allie muttered and parked the truck beside the curb. She jumped down and ran after Rylee, who glanced behind her and sped up.

She must have seen the fed-up gleam in her eyes. Allie wasn't afraid to put her hands on the tweaker.

When she reached Rylee, she clamped a hand on her shoulder.

Rylee spun and swung a fist toward her head, which Allie ducked beneath. But then she swung toward Allie's middle and connected with her belly.

"Oomph!" Allie saw red. It was like a wave that crashed over. Her face got hot, her fists clenched. She stepped forward and aimed a fist, but it was caught mid-air by a very large hand.

"Baby, I'll handle this."

Rylee was running again.

Animal caught up easily, snaked a hand around her waist, and drew her up against the side of his body. With her swinging, cussing, and kicking, he didn't pay her any mind, carrying her on his hip as he returned to Allie. "You okay, babe?"

She grimaced. "I wouldn't mind if you bounced her once or twice against the truck before you cuffed her."

"You're a bloodthirsty thing," he said, grinning.

She shook her head as he passed her on his way back to the truck. Then she watched as he lowered Rylee, forced her to face the truck, and quickly snapped handcuffs on her wrists. He opened the passenger side door and tossed her onto the seat. Then he raised a finger in warning. "Any more bullshit, and I'll hogtie you."

Rylee's shoulders slumped, but a smirk curled one side of her mouth as Allie gingerly stepped up into the truck.

AFTER THEY DROPPED Rylee at the jail, Animal drove Allie back to her 4Runner. She drove to the agency and made use of Brian's shower to clean up and change before the meeting.

A knock sounded on the door. "Allie, let me in."

She frowned at her reflection. She had yet to don her shirt. A spectacular bruise colored the center of her abdomen. She cracked open the door and stood to the side.

Animal stepped in and closed the door behind him. Then he knelt and touched her red and purple skin. "Ouch. How sore are you?"

"Hurts a little to breathe."

"She might have cracked a rib. Want to go to the hospital?"

"No, I'll be fine."

He stood and lifted her chin. "You should've let me handle her."

"Thought we already established, I'm not the patient kind," she grumbled.

He shook his head then reached for the chambray shirt she had hung on a hook beside the door.

She turned and let him slide the sleeves onto her arms, and then turned again to face him.

He swatted her hands away and began closing the buttons. "Want it tucked?" he asked, when he'd finished.

She shook her head then stepped closer to lean

her cheek against his shoulder. A huge sigh slipped out as he gently enclosed her within his arms.

"Fetch just arrived," he murmured.

"You tell him about Rylee?"

He grunted. "Guess I'm getting as gossipy as the rest of them."

A smile tugged at her mouth. "Imagine that."

"Lacey wanted to know why you looked so pale when you arrived."

She drew back and lifted her face.

He gave her the kiss she needed then dropped his arms. "The sooner we get this over with…"

"Yeah, can't wait to get back home."

He arched a brow.

"Your place," she quickly amended.

"Like the first way you described it. I've already asked for some time off to get you moved."

His voice was doing things to her. That soft rumble that passed for his whisper always sounded like a low growl. "I want you to grow your hair out."

He blinked, and then his mouth stretched into a sly smile. "What about my beard?"

"That too."

"Afraid I'm hiding a weak chin?"

She reached up and scratched her fingers through the hair covering his jaw. "No worries there. I just don't want you any more handsome. I'll have to fight off the women."

His chuckle gusted against her cheek. "I won't notice them. Only have eyes for you, baby."

She poked his side. "I'm going to have to stick close to home base to make sure of that."

"Won't hear me complaining."

She slipped her arms around his back and hugged him. Then she snuggled her face against his chest again. "I'm falling for you, Animal."

"Name's Russell," he whispered. "Russell Hathcoat."

Startled, she glanced up at him.

His dark gaze was solemn. "Just wanted to make sure you knew who you're in love with."

She laughed, and then moaned because it hurt. "Russ. I like that. But will you mind too much if I keep calling you Animal?"

"Why would you want to?"

"Because it's how I see you," she admitted. "You're a wild man. Especially when you make love to me."

His drew a deep breath and pulled on her braid. "I love you, too. I figured that out the first time you lifted your chin and gave me a mean glare."

"Did not."

"Did, too. Turned me the hell on."

She narrowed her eyes.

"Damn, don't do it," he growled. "I want a soft mattress under your back when I fuck you. Less jarring for those ribs."

Allie pouted but gave him a nod. "Let's go."

Everyone was gathered around Brian's big desk.

They perched on chairs and desks as she opened the files on her thumb drive.

They laughed as they watched the video of Animal running toward the mama bear. Her loud huffs and the sounds of her paws hitting the dirt as she warned him away, sent shivers down her back. She still couldn't believe he'd done that.

Then there were the shots she'd taken of the team, geared up and marching through the forest. The pictures caught not only the tone of the serious business the team conducted, but also the panorama of the settings—thick forests, dark ravines, towering mountains.

When she played the video of the encampment where they'd taken down Tibbets and his cousin, she watched their expressions. They were riveted, even though many of the crew had been there. Animal frowned, watching the way the feed jerked when she'd pitched to the side, capturing the canopy above, then settling, the audio capturing her surprised cry, the sounds of blows, and then showing the moment Animal knelt beside her, his features tight, then relaxing as he reached to touch the side of her head. "Baby, what'd you do?"

The women around her sighed. The men just shook their heads and chuckled softly.

She'd have been embarrassed to admit how many times she'd replayed it just to hear the way he'd said that. Lord, she'd loved him even then.

When she finished reviewing all the video and

stills with the team, she stood. "Well? Are you good with it?"

Fetch sat back in his chair and glanced around at the hunters. They all gave nods. When he turned to Allie, he smiled. "Mind if we pay for the use of some of this? Wouldn't have to be exclusive. I've been thinking we need more of a web presence, and these would work nicely. If you'd like to accompany us now and then, I'd probably buy more."

Pleased, she smiled. "I'd love to work with Brian on a blog. I know there will be privacy issues, so far as your skips are concerned, but there's a lot of good stuff here. I think people would love to see what you do."

Fetch pursed his lips and glanced at Brian. "Up to you, buddy."

Brian held out his hand to Allie. "Okay. That mean you're sticking around?"

Smiles stretched, and all gazes went to Animal.

His thick dark brows lowered. "Allie's moving in with me."

"Are you getting power sometime soon?" Fetch asked his eyes twinkling.

"Next week. I'm paying the electric company to put a rush on my order."

"I know a contractor..."

Allie shook her head. "We're doing the work," she said.

"At least the construction," Animal amended.

"We'll need a plumber and an electrician, but the rest is going to be up to us."

Fetch patted the arms of his chair and pushed up to stand. "Allie, you might want to make sure you're around the end of next week. We've got an ops van arriving. New tech we'll be using for the big jobs. I'd love some photos."

"I'll be here, camera ready," she said with a little salute.

The front door chime sounded and teenager wearing a Domino's shirt entered, his face hidden by the tall stack of pizza boxes he carried in his arms.

Lacey led him to the kitchen.

Allie pulled out the releases she'd brought for them to sign and handed them to Brian.

"I'll make sure all the Ts are crossed the Is dotted," he said.

"Thanks."

Brian's gaze locked with hers. "Sure you don't have a hunting bone in your body?"

"You mean, me become a bounty hunter?" She made a face as she rubbed her belly. "I prefer watching the action through my lens. I get close enough as it is."

Animal slid an arm around her. "Too close for my peace of mind."

"Huh" she said, tilting her head to meet his gaze. "Guess you'll have to keep me on a short leash."

"And I don't even want to know what that

means," Brian said, backing up his wheelchair. "Better get your pizza while it's hot."

"Let's eat," Animal said. "Then we'll continue this conversation back at the cabin."

She shivered at the hard edge of his voice. "Looking forward to it." Then she ducked away from his arm and ran for the kitchen.

CHAPTER 9

THE FIRST VIDEO uploaded to YouTube went viral inside seventy-two hours, thanks to a news anchor in L.A. who happened across the "Man Chasing Bear" video. Soon, all the major networks played it, and the newly launched website for Montana Bounty Hunters, which Fetch had envisioned as a selling tool to law enforcement agencies, had so many visitors that vendors selling tactical gear, clothing, and weapons asked to purchase advertising space. Allie now found herself selling sponsorships for the online articles and blogs she created for MBH. The Bear Lodge office, although only a satellite office of Montana Bounty Hunters, was now the face of the business Fetch had created.

After Allie posted the video of Tibbets's take-down, Hollywood called.

"We're sellouts," Reaper grumbled. "Animal, your girlfriend has created a monster."

"Speak for yourself," Lacey said, her bubbling enthusiasm a little jarring coming through Animal's earpiece. "Allie's letting me blog about what's inside my makeup bag when I go on a hunt. She's going to link it to *my* YouTube channel! I'm gonna be rich!"

Animal hunkered down behind a tree. He had a view of the northern side of the warehouse they were staking out. No doors, but a window large enough the "rats" inside might flee through it to escape. The sun had just set. The sky was overcast, further darkening his surroundings.

The team was fully "geared up". They wore Kevlar vests and helmets with night vision goggles attached. They were also heavily armed. Animal had a Glock in his holster and carried a Heckler & Koch G36 assault rifle. As soon as the power to the warehouse was cut, the team would make their move.

Everyone was tense. They'd rehearsed in an open field before they'd left their staging area. They knew their parts. Those with combat experience would enter the building. Carly and Lacey were safe inside the ops van, which sat a quarter mile away, ready to watch the live feeds from their helmets with Brian once they turned on the cameras. They'd watch for any problems and give them warnings.

Animal wasn't happy about it, but the TV crew and Allie were near enough that if any action spilled outside the warehouse, they'd film it.

Speaking of which, the film crew crashed through the forest behind him, the producer narrating in a mock whisper as he approached Animal's position. "Alone, surveilling the northside of the abandoned warehouse, Animal uses the skills he honed while serving as a Navy SEAL to conceal himself in the bushes..."

Animal glanced over his shoulder and aimed a glare at the cameraman. The crew would be with them for the next month to film. Then they'd head back to Hollywood to edit the shit out of whatever film they got to create a season's worth of stories for *Bounty Hunters of the Northwest.*

Animal worried that the hunters would end up being commercialized like the Duck Dynasty family, and he had no interest in seeing his face on blankets, pajamas, and men's boxers. Unfortunately, the producer seemed enamored with him. He'd seen the "Man Chasing Bear" video and loved it. He'd even had the nerve to ask Animal whether there was any chance he'd be willing to do "reenactments."

Hearing about that, Allie had laughed so hard, tears had streaked down her cheeks and she'd crossed her thighs to keep from peeing.

"We've got the road covered," came Dagger's voice. "No one coming in or out. Sheriff has deputies keeping us company, just in case they're needed."

Animal's heart began a slow, hard thud, like it did before every battle.

"Hey!" came Allie's voice. "I just zoomed in on the open door. I saw Parsons. He's talking to Junior and is wearing a navy hoodie. He's cut his hair, and it's bleached."

"Well, hallelujah," Reaper drawled. "Would've sucked if we'd brought everyone out here and he'd managed to slip the noose."

While digging around into Parsons's properties, the team had discovered that Parsons owned a warehouse near Poison. Although the pavement around it was crumbling and trees were growing into the fencing, the inside of the warehouse had looked far from abandoned. They'd found a vehicle, money bundled in plastic bags inside the trunk, and guessed rightly that he was planning his escape.

Out on a $350,000 bond, Parsons knew his chances of beating charges for interstate drug-trafficking were slim. His defense attorneys were working hard to bolster claims he only owned the semi-trucks that had been stopped for inspection by the highway patrol, and he wasn't responsible for what the operators hauled. However, his drivers had rolled to save their own hides. Parsons was looking at hard time.

Right now, Parsons, his son, and several of his "lieutenants" were inside the warehouse, no doubt making their plans to get to the coast. Brian had tracked Parsons' yacht to a marina near Seattle. The marina owner confirmed he'd refueled the boat, and that individuals had been in and out, stocking provisions.

Fetch had sent Wolf and Mace to the marina in

case Parsons escaped the team that had been watching him for days as he'd played golf at his country club, lunched with his lawyers, and made love to his much younger wife beside the backyard pool.

"Everybody should be in position," Brian said. "Turn on your cameras. Chime in to let me know you're ready."

Animal flicked on his goggles. One by one, the hunters answered.

"All right, boys," Fetch said once they'd finished. "We're a go. Reaper, cut the power. Team, move in!"

Seconds later, the lights inside the warehouse flickered out. As they'd rehearsed, the team cut fencing and moved with military precision to surround the building.

With the stock of his weapon hard against his shoulder, Animal moved toward the back window of the warehouse. Once there, he unclipped a stun grenade and crouched.

"Go, go, go!"

On Fetch's order, Animal popped up, broke the glass with the butt of his weapon, tossed the grenade inside, and hunkered down, hands over his ears.

Several explosions sounded from within, followed by shouts and short bursts of gunfire.

He bobbed up and glanced inside the cavernous building. The back of the warehouse was empty. After quickly clearing away the rest of the broken glass, he hung a padded mat over the edge and vaulted through the window. "I'm in the back," he said into his mike. "Moving forward." As planned, he kept close to the north side wall to avoid his own team's fire.

More bursts sounded. A figure holding a pistol in one hand crouched so low he looked to be half-crawling as he moved toward Animal.

Animal let him come up beside him then poked his ribs with his rifle. "Move and I'll fire," he growled.

The man's mouth dropped open, and he froze.

"Slide the gun away," he said, keeping his tone deadly even.

The weapon skated across the concrete floor. Animal stuck a knee in the center of the man's back, shouldered his weapon, and quickly ripped zip ties off his web belt to restrain the man's hands and feet before moving on.

Gunfire seemed to be centered around the walled-in office toward the front of the warehouse, so he moved toward the vehicles—the Land Rover that had been hidden there and the sedans Parsons' crew had parked a short time ago.

At the first sedan, he bent and looked beneath, then quickly scanned the interior. Empty. Again, he checked the second sedan but found no one hiding. Approaching the rear of the Land Rover, he saw boots sticking out from beneath the chassis. Again, shouldering his weapon, he reached down, grabbed the boots, and quickly slid the man out from under the car. The second he was clear, Animal straddled his body and pressed his hand against the back of the man's head to hold his face pressed to the concrete. "Don't move," he whispered next to his ear.

The man gurgled and held out his hands. Animal quickly restrained him then hauled him to his feet. With his fingers tugging on the zip tie, Animal guided the man between the vehicles then pushed him to his knees. "I have one tango tied in the back of the warehouse," he told the team. "Another by the Land Rover."

There was a lull in the gunfire.

"Three in the office," Reaper said. "They may be out of ammo."

Which accounted for all their targets.

"Norman Parsons," Fetch called out over the bullhorn. "We're Fugitive Recovery Agents. We have you surrounded. Two of your men are already in our custody. You, and the two in the office, come out with your hands over your heads."

Animal peered over at the office. In the grainy green light of his goggles, he watched as Parsons' son came out first, his hands high above his scrawny shoulders. Another man followed, his hand on the son's shoulder, likely because he couldn't see an inch ahead of him.

Last came Parsons with a scowl twisting his face and holding a hand against his upper arm.

"Get your hands up!" Reaper called out a warning.

"I'm fucking shot," Parsons said. "I'm bleeding!"

"Don't fucking care," Reaper said. "Get your hands up!"

Parsons winced and raised his hands.

"Calling for an ambulance," Brian said. "Someone get those lights on."

Moments later, the lights flickered on. Animal flipped up his goggles and blinked.

The team moved in, securing the men and gathering their weapons. With his pistol raised, Reaper ducked into the office to search it. "All clear," he called out.

Animal helped his prisoner stand then shoved him toward the large warehouse door. As he approached, the film crew crowded in front of him. Animal gave them a fierce frown and shouldered his way past them.

Outside, he waited as one of the deputy's vehicles rolled to a stop. "We'll take him from here," one deputy said as he approached. "Nice work, man."

Animal gladly handed him over then looked around the parking area.

From the darkness, Allie strode toward him. Her face was pale as her gaze searched his face then raked over his frame. When she looked up again, a crooked smile lifted one side of her mouth.

Animal opened his arms, and she ran to him, thudding against his body. "That wasn't as much fun as I thought it would be," she said, her voice muffled by his chest.

He nuzzled her hair. "You and the film crew

were supposed to wait until the 'all clear'. Fetch hasn't called it yet."

"Huh. Got tired of waiting."

Animal stood holding her for the longest time, waiting for her to stop shivering and his heart to quiet.

"All clear," Fetch said at last, "Brian, Dagger, you can roll in now."

When Allie finally leaned away and looked up at him, he bent and kissed her hard. "Best way to end an op—ever," he said, fisting her hair then diving down for one more kiss.

"Allie!" Lacey called out.

Animal glanced toward the van as Lacey leapt from the passenger seat to the ground and ran toward them. "Wait until you see the feeds from their helmets! We're going to get so many hits!"

"More than your makeup bag video?" Allie teased.

Animal kept his arm around her back as the rest of the team gathered. The deputies had the prisoners. Reaper stayed beside Parsons. Someone would have to ride with him to the hospital to wait until he got patched up before they delivered him to lockup.

Fetch strode toward the group, a wide smile stretching his mouth. "Great job, everyone! After you turn your helmets over to Brian, the deputies will want your statements. We're not done yet."

Allie groaned and leaned into Animal's body.

He bent toward her ear. "Yeah. Can't wait to get you back to our place."

"Damn," she whispered. "You have no idea how bad I want you right now."

"We hear you," Reaper said, his voice sounding wry in his ear.

Allie's eyes widened. "Forgot about these," she said, reaching up to remove her device.

Around them, all the hunters laughed.

ANIMAL'S BODY TIGHTENED. His breath caught. Once again, he staggered to his feet. He shook his head, sounds coming in muffled, his head spinning. He didn't want to look around. He knew what he would see. What he always saw.

Another explosion shook the ground. The sand beneath his feet seemed to shiver. Smoke drifted past his face. If he glanced back, he'd see them. His teammates. His friends.

Jesus, not again.

But before he could force himself to turn, something changed. Soft hands encircled his waist. A weight clung to his back.

"Animal, wake up, baby. Wake up."

He blinked and opened his eyes to the darkness. It took a moment to process where he was. Not the sunny camp in the desert with body parts strewn like garbage. His bedroom in the cabin.

He dragged in a deep breath and turned his head. "I'm awake," he said, his voice croaking.

"Bad dream?" she asked softly.

He nodded then cleared his throat. "Yes."

"You went stiff, and you moaned. Woke me up."

"Sorry." He rubbed a hand over his face, taking the moment to gather his composure. Then he turned and gathered her into his arms. "If it happens again," he said, "you might want to move out of the bed."

"Do you think you'll hurt me?"

"I don't know. Sometimes, I wake up with my hands curled into fists. I could."

She rested against his chest and placed a hand alongside his cheek. "Have you talked to anybody about this?"

"You mean, a shrink?"

Her nod shifted her hair against his skin.

"No." He drew a deep breath. "But I will."

"Brian's friend, Raydeen. Bet she knows someone."

"I'll ask her."

"Anytime you want to talk..."

He closed his eyes. "I know." But he didn't like thinking about that day, much less describing it to someone else. And he hated sharing that ugliness with her. That sorrow. Not when they were doing so well, and he was feeling happier than he'd ever felt. "I love you, Allie."

"Just know I'm here for you. Whatever you need."

"What I need," he said, "is you. Here. Always."

She touched his chin. "When this house is done," she said, "I want to marry you."

He cleared his throat. "You asking me?"

"Nope. Telling."

While her tone was teasing, she held her breath. He knew what she was doing. Distracting him from his memories.

Without warning her, he rolled over her, trapping her beneath his body. He slid one knee between her legs and then the other, forcing her open.

Her hands went to his hair, and her fingers raked his scalp.

Without lifting his torso, he rooted his rapidly hardening cock between her legs. When he found her entrance, he pushed, entering her.

Her breath hissed between her teeth. "I'll never tire of how that feels."

"What? My big-ass cock?"

She giggled. "Yeah. I always have a second, when I'm sure there's no way you'll fit, and then you're in. Takes my breath."

He framed her face inside his hands. "I'm going to fuck you hard, Allie Travers."

"Promises, promises," she murmured.

He growled and raised himself to his elbows.

Allie lifted her legs and rubbed her thighs against his sides, letting him stroke deeper. Her fingers scratched over his back.

He growled again and leaned down to rub his

face against her shoulder. "*Jesus, fuck,* you feel so good."

"Um, not that I want you to stop, but we forgot something," she said, moaning.

"Didn't forget a damn thing," he said. "No more fucking rubbers. I only wanna feel you." He'd save the rubbers for a different kind of play—once she got over being shy.

Her inner muscles squeezed around him, and he groaned. "Do it again."

When she squeezed him again, he moved faster, glorying in her slippery heat.

For months, he'd thought he wanted to be alone. That he didn't deserve any happiness. But now, he realized that crawling into a dark place wasn't the way to honor his friends. Animal was ready to move on and live his life. He'd make a family with this woman and embrace the new adventures they'd find along the way.

Faster and faster, he moved, until his balls tingled and his breath hitched. He gritted his teeth. Just one second more.

Then Allie's soft cries floated around him, filling him with joy. With one last downward swoop to kiss her, he brought them home.

S*X ON THE BEACH

A SEALS IN PARADISE/MONTANA BOUNTY HUNTERS CROSSOVER STORY

New York Times and *USA Today* Bestselling Author
Delilah Devlin

New York Times & USA Today Bestselling Author
DELILAH DEVLIN
HOT SEAL
S*X
on the
BEACH
SEALS
in
Paradise

CHAPTER ONE

Six months ago...

Carson "Beach-boy" Walsh pulled his dog tags from under his shirt, and then exposed the small medallion that rested against one rubber-clad tag, lifted it to his mouth, and kissed it.

So, Saint Christopher wasn't actually considered a saint anymore, and Carson wasn't Catholic, but his aunt had given him the medallion the first time he'd shipped out. Kissing it for luck before a fight had become a ritual.

After tucking the medal back inside his shirt, he raised his MK17 to hold it crosswise in front of his body as he continued the march into the valley. He breathed in through his nose and out through his mouth to calm his heart and head. Another part of his "pre-game" ritual.

He was on his fifteenth deployment, and he'd lost

count of how many missions. He'd just hit his ten-year mark as a SEAL, and he was one lucky guy. Everyone said so. Other than a little shrapnel and splinters, he'd never been seriously injured.

Sure, he'd had a moment during his thirteenth deployment, when he thought maybe he'd run out of luck—when he'd stepped on a landmine. But the second his boot had landed on the metal plate buried in the sand, he'd known exactly what was happening, and had pitched himself over a stone wall a split-second before it exploded, a *luckily* delayed reaction, which had showered him with dirt. His buddies had rushed to him, certain they'd be picking up pieces of his body, but he'd sat up, shook his head, and grinned.

"Goddamn, Beach-boy," his best buddy Fischer had said as he slapped his back. "You are one lucky bastard."

Yeah, that had been his closest call, but he didn't take his luck for granted. He trained hard, kept alert to his surroundings, and trusted the men on his team. *They* were the source of his real luck.

He'd lost friends along the way, to death and career-ending injuries. He knew, someday, his streak would end, but it wouldn't be today. Not this early morning when the sun was painting the prettiest dawn as it climbed over the rim of the valley. Bright yellow at the edge, a pale purple and orange just above it. While he preferred a bit more greenery, the sparse bushes and trees dotting the rocky valley below looked almost lush compared to the countryside they'd been quickly moving through. The walled compound below looked like a crumbling castle from some ancient tale. A castle they hoped contained their current target, an insurgent leader who'd escaped a series of raids, and who'd publicly mocked his would-be captors.

The team was eager to capture Ahmadi, who'd become a kind of superstar, even among those who wanted to see an end to the Taliban's reign of terror, once and for all. They admired the fact he'd managed to survive, always staying one step ahead of his American pursuers.

When they reached the outer wall of the compound, Carson paused as his team moved past. Every one of them reached out a hand to rub his helmet, their own lucky ritual, before they took positions along the wall. Carson was on point. He'd be the first inside the compound—after he blew the thick plank door set into the wall.

Fischer rubbed his helmet then took a knee beside the door. "Don't get killed."

"You can have my helmet if I do," Carson said with a quick, tight grin. Then he reached out, stuck the small explosive charge next to the lock on the door, set the timer, and then took cover.

He counted the seconds and covered his ears. As soon as the C-4 exploded, he pushed up and ran quickly through the opening, heading toward the side of the mud-stuccoed house in the center of the open compound. As he moved, the only sounds were the quiet crunches of boots behind him. Not a bleat from a goat, not a bark from a dog, not a shout. "Too damn quiet," he said.

"Damn, I hope he hasn't already slipped the noose," the mission commander said in his earpiece. "Breach the door, but keep your eyes peeled."

"Anyone tell him that never sounds good?" Fischer muttered.

Hunkered down with his weapon raised, the buttstock snug against his shoulder, Carson kept close to the wall as he moved toward the alcove shading the front door. He checked the dirt around the concrete porch but saw no signs of recent digging, so no mines, he hoped. Then he ducked into the alcove, Fischer right behind him, his back to Carson as he continued to scan their surroundings.

Carson moved to the door, reached out with his left hand, and pulled down on the latch. He heard a snick, but also a snap. His heart thudded, and he turned to Fischer, "Go, go, g—"

An explosion sounded behind him, a millisecond before the door slammed into his back and pushed him ahead of a blast of fire and air that picked him and Fischer up. When he landed, he scrambled toward his buddy. Fischer lay face down, his arms spread.

Sounds around him were muffled—pops of gunfire, distant shouts. He crawled to Fischer and gently rolled him over. His face was covered in sand

and grit...and blood, seeping from beneath his helmet. No, his ear.

"Fisch," he shouted close to him, but Fischer didn't stir.

"Man down. Fisch is down," he said into his mic, but couldn't hear a response. Sounds faded. He knelt, knowing he couldn't do a thing—not remove his friend's helmet, not move him again. He swayed on his knees and nearly fell, but more of his team arrived, pulling him away, running their hands over his back.

He sucked a breath between his teeth when he felt a sudden sharp pain on the right side of his back. More muffled voices shouted into his ear. "Lie down, Walsh! Helo's coming!"

At that moment, Carson realized his luck had just run out. Too soon to save Fischer. Maybe too soon to save himself.

Three months ago...

The sky was blue, the temperature was in the mid-seventies, and a light breeze filtered through the leaves of the cottonwoods. It was a gorgeous, glorious Montana day, and Gina Tripp was pumped. Her boss, Fetch Winter, had finally let go of the tight leash he'd kept her on since he'd hired her after she'd left active duty where they first met. Before he'd mustered out, he'd given her his number and told if ever she needed a job...

She'd accepted his offer and moved to Montana from her home in San Diego. So far, she loved the climate, the mountains, the people she worked with, and, especially, the job. Bounty hunting was damn fun, and from listening to the stories of the more experienced hunters, she was eager to experience the occasional adrenaline rush she'd grown addicted to in the Army. But she was the "new girl" and had to prove herself before they'd trust her with the scary shit.

The past two weeks, Fetch had finally let her take solo baby-steps—rounding up druggies who'd missed their court-ordered drug tests, picking up an old Buick from a seventy-year-old woman who'd signed away her car to bail out her deadbeat son, only to have him skip his date with the judge.

Nothing big. Nothing dangerous. She'd performed well on other tasks, working the phones to give the other hunters leads. At last, Fetch was trusting her to serve as part of the team going after Harland Oates, a once-convicted felon, who hadn't been seen since he'd met his bail for a DUI offense that he'd compounded by assaulting the arresting officer.

Gina had "geared up" along with two other hunters from the Kalispell office, Sam Meacham and "Kid" Hagerty. *They* were armed with handguns, a rifle, and a pellet gun. She'd been given beanbag rounds for her shotgun, something non-lethal because the men were nervous she'd shoot them by mistake.

She'd snorted at that assumption, but they'd taken her new nickname "Trip" to heart. So, she'd faceplanted on the drive outside the office during an ice storm. And once, she'd slid like surfer across a sheet of black ice during a coffee run, only to hit hard snow and somersault. After managing to save one lidded drink, she'd thought that would count for something.

Nope. They'd taken the security camera footage and posted it on YouTube. Now, she was known as the Calamity Jane of the bounty hunting world, at least here in Montana.

Fetch had told her to stop trying so hard. *Relax.* She'd eventually find her feet in the job. She'd rolled her eyes, and he'd laughed at his joke. He predicted, that in the end, she'd be a hell of a hunter.

But her training was taking a little longer than she liked. Like most of the people he'd hired, she was ex-military. She'd seen action as a driver in Iraq, driving in convoys transporting supplies across huge expanses of open desert. She'd had to bail out of a 5-ton truck a time or two to set up a quick defense against attacks from ISL forces. She'd even shot her weapon. Not that she'd ever hit a thing. Didn't matter. She'd done her job. Had been prepared for worst case scenarios. She knew how to solider, how to follow orders, and she didn't lose her nerve when things got grim.

She reminded herself of all these things as she trudged behind Sam and Kid toward a house, of sorts, deep inside the woods. The structure had begun its life as a school bus but had been "renovated" with wood-framed offshoots that sat on piers that looked like a stiff wind would shift them right off their foundations. This was Harland's "hunting cabin" or so his buddies back at the bar in Bozeman had said.

Gina's Kevlar vest was a little large, and the top rubbed the underside of her chin. She reached for the bottom edge and tugged it down to just above her hips, and then hurried to catch up with the guys on the trail.

They both turned and shot her harsh glares, but she gave them a smile. Kill them with kindness; that was her motto. They likely thought she was a bit of a snowflake she smiled so damn much.

Kid had already asked her on a date, but she'd told him she didn't think it was a good idea—at least not until she was off her ninety-day probation. She had to be all about the job. Still, turning him down had been hard. The man was beautiful, although she was sure he wouldn't like being described that way, but he did have the dreamiest gray-blue eyes, soot-black wavy hair that he kept cut short, and a body that any breathing woman, and probably a lot of men, would sigh over.

But it was better to keep her mind on the job, not the way his Levi jeans hugged his ass. When she headed back to California for her best friend's wedding, she'd be sure to scout out a booty call to take care of any unrequited urges Kid inspired.

"Trip!" came a harsh whisper in her earpiece.

She glanced up and caught Sam's signal. They'd circled to the back of the ramshackle cabin, and Kid had his back to the siding as he edged closer to a window to peek inside.

"He's inside. Kitchen," Kid whispered then ducked down.

Sam caught her glance, pointed toward the back door, and made some sort of hand signal. Not strictly military, so she wasn't exactly sure if he was telling her to guard it or open it, but she nodded and moved toward the rickety back steps. When he disappeared around the front of the structure, she guessed she was supposed to wait, because he'd likely be the one to breach the front door. She edged quietly up the wooden steps to stand at the back door.

"Harland Oates, Fugitive Recovery Agents!"

Gina winced at the shout in her ear, but then almost snickered at the way Sam had said the felon's name. It had sounded like "Hall & Oats" and, not for the first time, she was tempted to break out in song. "Maneater" came to mind.

"We have your place surrounded! Come out with your hands up!" A moment passed. "I'm goin' in!" Sam whispered.

A crash sounded in the distance. Footsteps pounded through the bus, striking metal then wood. Then the knob on the door in front of her twisted. She only had a second to jerk back into the tiny space behind the door as it slammed open. When a man began to emerge, all she saw was wild hair, a wilder beard, and bare muscled arms.

Has to be Harland. Fuck! She pushed the door back as hard as she could against the large body hurtling out onto the porch.

She caught him, sort of.

Harland Oates slammed against the railing. "What the fuck!"

The porch shuddered then teetered to the side. She grabbed for Harland, caught his grubby wifebeater in her fist, but he fell through the rail, taking her with him. They landed on the ground, her body bouncing against his back, her shotgun banging against his head. When she scrambled to her knees, she was straddling him and fighting to get her shotgun turned in the small space between their bodies, when he bucked upward, sending her to the side.

Still turning the weapon, her finger got stuck in the trigger housing and a round went off, pounding into the ground beside his head, and he froze.

They both turned their gazes to the expended round. The lead-filled red "pillow" was disintegrated.

"Bitch, you almost shot me in the fucking head!" Harland whined.

It took everything not to blurt that it had been an accident. Instead, she gave him her meanest stare. "You gonna give me any more trouble?"

"Trip, what the hell?" Sam shouted from the back door.

She glanced up to see him tip back his cowboy hat. He couldn't step out because the porch had collapsed. "We're good, Sam," she said, then dragged the muzzle of her shotgun closer to Harland's belly. "Ain't that right?"

Harland groaned and wilted against the dirt just as Kid strode to her side.

Sam shook his head and disappeared back inside, his feet clomping through the cabin.

Kid offered his hand. "Not exactly graceful, are you, Trip?"

She squinted up at him. "If you ever want that date, you better take that back. I got him, didn't I?"

His mouth stretched into a huge grin. "Wish I'd had a camera. You should have seen your face when that porch fell out from under you." He glanced down at Harland who'd reached out his hands, showing he was ready to surrender.

"Can ya get off me now?" Harland asked.

Kid cupped her elbow and grabbed her shotgun, holding it well away as he helped her to her feet. "I got this. Don't want you to get those fingers stuck again."

"They weren't stuck," she lied, her cheeks feeling as though they were on fire.

"Sure, and you meant to knock him out with the door, right?"

"I don't suppose you could keep the after-action report to 'Trip took down the target', could you?"

He gave her a sly wink. "Oh, that's exactly what happened, wasn't it?"

Her shoulders fell. No way in hell would either of the hunters let her live this one down. She'd be stuck relieving grannies of their prized possessions for the rest of her days.

"Make yourself useful and get him cuffed before Sam gets here," he said.

As she drew her handcuffs from the pocket on her web belt, Kid pulled out his cellphone from under his vest.

While he took pictures of the collapsed steps, she helped Harland to his feet. The man wasn't very tall. She probably could have taken him from behind if she'd let him climb down the steps first. Instead, adrenaline had been her bitch.

As she led him back through the woods to their SUV, she heard laughter following her every step of the way.

ABOUT DELILAH DEVLIN

Delilah Devlin is a *New York Times* and *USA TODAY* bestselling author with a reputation for writing deliciously edgy stories with complex characters. She has published nearly two hundred stories in multiple genres and lengths, and she is published by Atria/Strebor, Avon, Berkley, Black Lace, Cleis Press, Ellora's Cave, Entangled, Grand Central, Harlequin Spice, HarperCollins: Mischief, Kensington, Montlake Romance, Running Press, and Samhain Publishing.

You can find Delilah all over the web:
WEBSITE
BLOG
TWITTER
FACEBOOK FAN PAGE
PINTEREST

Subscribe to her newsletter **so you don't miss a thing!**

Or email her at: delilah@delilahdevlin.com

Montana Bounty Hunters

Reaper (#1)

Dagger (#2)

Reaper's Ride (#3)

Cochise (#4)

Hook (#5)

Wolf (#6)

Animal (#7)

S*x on the Beach (related)

Uncharted SEALs

Watch Over Me (#1)

Her Next Breath (#2)

Through Her Eyes (#3)

Dream of Me (#4)

Baby, It's You (#5)

Before We Kiss (#6)

Between a SEAL and a Hard Place (#7)

Heart of a SEAL (#8)

Hard SEAL to Love (#9)

Big Sky SEAL (#10)

Head Over SEAL (#11)

SEAL Escort (#12)

Texas Cowboys

Wearing His Brand (#1)

The Cowboys and the Widow (#2)

Soldier Boy (#3)

Bound & Determined (#4)

Slow Rider (#5)

Night Watch (#6)

Triplehorn Brand

Laying Down the Law (#1)

In Too Deep (#2)

A Long, Hot Summer (#3)

Night Fall

Sm{B}itten (#1)

Truly, Madly...Deadly (#2)

Knight in Transition (#3)

Wolf in Plain Sight (#4)

Knight Edition (#5)

Night Fall on Dark Mountain (#6)

Frannie and the Private Dick (#7)

Sweet Succubus (#8)

Truly, Madly...Werely (#9)

Bad to the Bone (#10)

Long Howl Good Night (#11)

First Knight (#12)

Big Bad Wolf (#13)

Texas Billionaires Club

Tarzan & Janine (#1)

Something To Talk About (#2)

Who's Your Daddy (#3)

Love & War (#4)

Some Standalone Stories

Begging For It

Hot Blooded

Raw Silk

Warrior's Conquest

Rogues

Enslaved by the Viking Short Story

Conquests

Smokin' Hot Firemen